THE AMERICAN MUSICAL THEATRE:

A Manual for Performers
A Guide for Authors, Directors, Producers,
Educators and Students

A Complete Musical Theatre Course

Steven Porter, Ph.D.

Dir. of Music, City Schools of Binghamton, N.Y.

BARCLAY HOUSE ● New York, N.Y.

THE AMERICAN MUSICAL THEATRE

By STEVEN PORTER

Published by:
Barclay House
15 West 44th St., New York, N.Y. 10036

Typesetting, music engraving and layouts by:
Excelsior Typographers and Engravers, Unltd.

First Edition

Library of Congress Cataloging-in-Publication Data

Porter, Steven, 1943-
    The American musical theatre.

    Bibliography: p.
    Includes index.
    1. Musical revue, comedy, etc. 2. Musical revue,
comedy, etc.--Production and direction. I. Title.
ML1950.P68 1987   782.81   87-14495
ISBN O-935016-97-X

To Elaine Kuracina

★*actress and friend*★

To Laurence Wren —
For the love of musical
theatre —

Elaine Kuracina

Table of Contents

Part IV

Trying Your Hand

PREFACE

From my childhood in a theatrical household, through many years of school classes and productions, from the wit and wisdom of Lehman Engel at the BMI Workshop to countless musicals as a director, I have gained an ever-increasing awareness of the plight of American Musical Theatre performers.

For years they have trooped into their auditions, hearts in their mouths, desperate to try, hopeful of success, longing for the recognition which can feed the fire they feel inside. And often, well-intentioned and talented as they are, they come to the task ill-prepared, not so much by choice, but because their education has in many cases failed them.

You can probably count on your fingers and toes the number of American secondary schools which offer courses in the Musical Theatre. It is only recently that American colleges have given performers a chance to major in Musical Theatre, and there are not many which do that—at least in comparison with other disciplines. And often, the instruction which does exist is woefully inadequate either because the course content is poor or the teaching less than first-rate.

The remedy for the problem is, of course, knowledge. Knowledge provides not only the power to be excellent but the protection which every Musical Theatre performer must have in order to survive. Protection against what, you ask? The director who doesn't understand his material; the librettist who produces banality in place of profundity; the composer who has never sung what he expects others to sing; the producer whose disorganization gives you three days of run-throughs when three weeks are needed; the publisher who disseminates arias in the wrong key; the conductor who asks you to shriek over the brasses instead of lowering their volume or re-scoring the accompaniment; the set designer who makes entrances difficult when they could be easy; the costumer who gives you a five-piece change in a two-minute break.

With the hope that it can fill in some of the gaps, this book is divided into four parts, each of which is critical to the development of the performer.

Part I is a brief history of the American Musical Theatre, for it is only in the context of history that the material on which you work can be fully judged and mastered.

Part II is a brief discussion of the elements of production. Knowing what ought to take place in a well-planned show can go a long way toward counteracting what does not take place in a poorly planned one.

Part III is a brief discussion of how to evaluate the elements of craftmanship one expects to find in the writing and performing of a musical. The knowledge here is indispensable to the performer. It is the feel of the plane to the pilot, the touch of the key to the pianist. It is, in fact, the very life blood of the art form.

Finally, Part IV provides an opportunity to put into practice what previous study has taught. Here, the student will write, produce, and perform material for the musical stage.

In describing the format above, I repeatedly use the word "brief" for a reason. Extensive historical studies, extended courses in creative writing and/or musical composition, performance workshops for the actor and singer are all things requiring far more time and depth than any one course or one volume can provide. The object here is an overview of the Musical Theatre which integrates the elements of historical understanding, production, writing, and performance. It is meant as a foundation upon which deeper and more detailed study may be safely built.

It is equally important to note that the title of this text uses the word "workbook." At no point should the text degenerate into reading which is not applied to the task of actual performance, actual discussion, actual writing. Therefore, liberally scattered through each part are assignments, suggested listenings, and topics for discussion—things without which no relevant text or serious student could exist.

Lastly, I would like to direct your attention to the words "musical" and "American." Exactly what constitutes a "musical" is somewhat open to debate. Is *'Porgy and Bess'* a "musical" or an "opera?" Indeed, what is the difference? And what of *'West Side Story'* or *'The Threepenny Opera?'* Are they musicals? Does a study of them belong here? My basic attitude regarding questions like these is to be more broad than narrow in definitions. For me, there is little difference between an operetta, a musical comedy, and a musical play—though each term, as you will see, has come into favor during one historical era or another. The sharp distinction I make is between opera on the one hand and all other forms of Musical Theatre on the other—and even that is somewhat arbitrary.

For the purposes of this text, I consider opera to be Musical Theatre with all or most of its dialogue sung. Such composition—the work of Handel, of Scarlotti, of Mozart and Gluck, Rossini, Verdi, Wagner, Puccini, Berg, or Britten—is not the work we will study here. Nor is my definition all that good, for we will include *'Porgy and Bess'* with sung dialogue and not include Mozart's *Magic Flute,* a singspiel opera with some spoken dialogue. Consider the definition as "workable" if not "immutable," and accept the works discussed as "the American Musical Theatre."

Which leads us to the word "American." Musical Theatre has rich traditions both in European opera which can be safely traced to the city of Florence around 1600, and in the Music Halls of England which flourished as early as the eighteenth century. But apart from the London stage, it has been America—particularly New York's Broadway—which has contributed the great bulk of the genre we will study here. It is therefore fitting that we label our product accordingly. Let us agree that we will concentrate on those shows which played in America under the general heading "musical" from about 1890 onward. Indeed, that will be quite enough.

Reader's note: Musicals are in italics and single quotes. Other major works are in italics only. Song titles are in quotes but not italicized.

Steven Porter
1986

PART I

A Brief History
Of The
American Musical

A. FOUNDATIONS AND BEGINNINGS

It is difficult to say exactly where the American musical was born. To claim any one event, any one production, as a definitive starting point would more than likely slight another equally worthy choice. Let us, then, be both egalitarian and non-controversial and say that the American musical had several wellsprings which justify our attention.

The earliest musical production in the American Colonies of which we have more or less precise accounts was an English ballad opera called *Flora*, presented in Charleston, South Carolina in 1735. It was done with no scenery or costumes and was in reality a spoken play with preexisting popular songs interspersed amid the dialogue. The use of preexisting musical material was by no means unusual. It would be done many more times before the practice of writing plays with original music would come into fashion.

The colonial years, ones of Revolution and political purpose, were not conducive to great theatrical development. There was simply more pressing business on the national agenda. One popular form of the late eighteenth and early nineteen century which did find some recognition, however, was the musical parody. A great play or poem, a noted story or famous performer would become the object of a humorous satire, often performed as a pantomime with songs and dances thrown in to provide both entertainment and variety. Such productions were called "burlesques," a genre not to be confused with the girly shows of the next century. One of the most successful burlesques of this era was the 1828 parody of Shakespeare's *Hamlet* starring the well-known British performer, John Poole.

If the burlesque and imported musical were popular, they also lacked the vital ingredient of any indigenous national musical form—originality. A burgeoning America needed something natively American to complement the influences of Europe and fire its own creative juices. That something was the Minstrel Show.

The Minstrel Show was a product of the black slave culture and its intermingling with a white colonial potpourri. It was the first major contribution of blacks to the American musical mainstream and by no means the last. But the Minstrel Show was also the product of a solitary man who gave it shape, architecture, and notoriety. The man was Dan Emmett. In 1843, Emmett brought his Virginia Minstrels to the Chatham Square Theatre of New York where they performed a show whose format would become a standard theatrical product from one end of the new republic to the other.

Emmett (the composer of such song classics as "Old Dan Tucker" and "The Blue Tail Fly") divided his show into three parts. Part one was known as the "olio." Here, the performers—bedecked in black face and wearing blue swallowtail coats, striped shirts, and pantaloons—would troop out and sit in a straight line across the stage. On one end of the line was the character of Mr. Tambo; on the other end, the character of Mr. Bones; in the middle, Mr. Interlocutor. The characters would

3.

carry on snappy banter, pausing in their humorous dialogue to allow one or another member of the line to rise and perform some kind of musical offering, a song or dance or entertaining routine. Occasionally, the entire ensemble would do some sort of chorus number.

When the olio was over, part two, the "fantasia," began. During the fantasia, individual star performers appeared with extended routines. Just who would be highlighted in a fantasia depended upon the make-up of the ensemble. If the company had a prodigious dancer, then dancing would dominate the fantasia; if a prodigious singer, then singing; etc.

Following the fantasia, the entire ensemble would appear in part three, a burlesque (parody) satirizing one or another of the earlier routines.

Emmett's formula was duplicated by many other minstrel groups, the most famous of which was the Ed Christy Minstrel Show for whom Stephen Foster wrote some of his best-known songs ("The Old Folks at Home" and "My Old Kentucky Home," to name just two). As Christy and his counterparts toured about, they engrained the Minstrel Show format into the country's theatrical consciousness, and it would be difficult to underestimate the influence of the format on later musical productions. The olio grew to become the variety or vaudeville show; the fantasia became the Broadway revue. The musical burlesque expanded to the dimension of full satire and gave rise to such later musicals as Stephen Sondheim's *'A Funny Thing Happened on the Way to the Forum'* (1962) and Leonard Bernstein's *'Candide'* (1956).

Minstrel Shows were staples of the American Musical Theatre as long as the population centers of the nation were rural. Rural populations meant traveling shows, shows which were mobile, which could reach out and find an audience here, an audience there. When the demography began to shift—as it did between 1850 and 1900—the theatrical landscape changed along with it. As cities became larger, they could afford to attract and support permanent theatres and non-traveling entertainment. It is not surprising, therefore, that the second half of the nineteenth century saw other genres join the Minstrel Show in the American musical mainstream.

In 1866 *'The Black Crook'* opened in New York City. Dramatically, it told in a rather confused and elongated plot of an evildoer who makes a bargain with the devil to deliver one human soul per year. But the contrived drama bothered very few people, for it was merely the literary excuse for the real point of the production, extravagance. For five and one half hours, *'The Black Crook'* paraded across the stage an array of theatrical effects and sensual pleasures the likes of which Broadway had never before seen. Simulated hurricanes, demonic rituals, extended ballets, angels ascending and descending in chariots of gold, scantily-clad chorus girls singing songs of sexual innuendo like "You Naughty, Naughty Men"—all this and more bedazzled the average theatre-goer. The theatrical extravaganza was born.

'The Black Crook' ran for four hundred performances, showed an initial profit of over one million dollars, and in revivals ran for another two thousand performances—figures unheard of at the time. The effect of the show was enormous, not because it catapulted musical theatre into the realm of big business, or because it spawned many imitations in the years which followed, but because it showed producers and investors alike that theatrical frivolity could profitably substitute for dramatic or musical substance.

In our brief historical excursion, we will see this phenomenon occur again and again, as indeed it is occurring on Broadway at the time of this writing. In the absence of well-crafted music, of meaningful characterization or profound thematic plot, it is historically Broadway's preference to substitute the effects of theatrical technology, the titillations of overt sexuality, the shocks of the bizarre. In the post 1970 era, one can point to shows like *'Cats,' 'Little Shop of Horrors,' 'Sweeney Todd,' 'La Cage Aux Follies,'* and many more as evidence that the legacy of *'The Black Crook'* is still with us.

In 1874 *'Evangeline'* opened in New York City. A burlesque by E.E. Rice on the Longfellow poem, *'Evangeline'* was the first production for which the entire musical score was newly composed. Previously, while some musical numbers might be written for opening night, most songs were preexisting pieces merely interpolated into the story at hand. Now a new pattern would emerge, the libretto accompanied by entirely original musical material. Not coincidentally, *'Evangeline'* was billed by its author as a new kind of work, a work he called "musical comedy."

Now that Broadway had seen the birth of a permanently located extravaganza and an originally composed musical score, it was only fitting that it see an original libretto as the dramatic underpinning of a musical production. The year was 1879; the show, Nate Salisbury's *'The Brook.'* Salisbury set his story at a picnic which has attracted a variety of people, each of whom is followed in a series of plots and subplots united by the common thread of the picnic and the brook which flows along the picnic grounds.

The use of a common event or common locale to interweave the separate stories of different characters has, during the 1980's, seen something of a theatrical explosion, particularly on television. For years, daytime TV soap operas have used the device, but more recently, nighttime shows like *Dallas, Knots Landing, Dynasty,* and *Falcon Crest* have attempted to capitalize on the formula. In the realm of the stage musical, *'Sunday in the Park with George'* was a recent attempt to unite the separate stories of the various characters in Seurat's famous pointilistic painting of a park scene.

For the most part, libretti like that of *'The Brook'* and *'Sunday in the Park with George'* are condemned by their very nature to remain fragmented and thematically shallow. Trying to weave a unified plot or express a unified theme with characters who are brought together more by superficial ruses than by substantive interaction is nigh on impossible, and in a later chapter we will discuss the weakness of such construction in more detail. For now it is important only to note that Salisbury's format bears historical significance not only because it was imitated one hundred years later, but because it brought to the American Musical Theatre a concern and desire for a dramatically meaningful story.

That desire continued to express itself during the 1880's in a series of productions known as the "Mulligan Shows," perhaps the most famous of which was *'The Mulligan Guard'* which opened in 1879. Text and lyrics by Ed Harrigan and Tony Hart, original music by David Braham, the show was a burlesque on the common people of New York. An Irish family, the Mulligans, repleat with melting pot neighbors and a Negro maid, were the focal point of the story, and through them, tales of the ordinary were dignified and raised to the level of theatrical centrality. Not so much for their own worth, but rather for their historical contribution, the Mulligan shows bear mention, for in the golden age of the musical theatre to come, the common man would again and again be cast as the central character. Tevye in *'Fiddler on the Roof,'*

Liza Doolittle in *'My Fair Lady,'* Tony and Maria in *'West Side Story'* all owe a portion of their existence to the Mulligan shows.

Finally, the years between the Civil War and the "Gay '90's" saw the advent of a kind of musical theatre which would grow to dominate the scene until 1920 and beyond—the operetta.

Now that populations could support permanent theatres; now that original music, original story, and opulent productions were viable; America was ready for the influences of Europe. From the early Italian masters of 1600 to the genius of Mozart, Verdi, Wagner, and many more, Europe had built an unrivaled legacy of serious grand opera. Now, during the second half of the nineteenth century, it complemented that legacy with a lighter but no less grand form of musical theatre. Through composers like Jacques Offenbach and Johann Strauss, in works like *The Tales of Hoffmann* and *Die Fledermaus,* European operetta reached a zenith, and when it played to audiences in the New World, it was an instant success. Particularly popular were the satiric operettas of Gilbert and Sullivan. When *The Mikado* and *H.M.S. Pinafore* toured the country, they generated enormous support and spawned many home-grown imitations.

Willard Spencer's *'The Little Tycoon'* (1886); John Philip Sousa's *'El Capitan'* (1896); and *'Robin Hood,'* the 1890 production by Reginald de Koven and H.B. Smith which sported the classic wedding song "Oh Promise Me;" each ran extensively as America's contribution to the world of operetta. But it was one man above all others who would epitomize the new form—epitomize it, and bring the nation into a new era of musical theatre. The man was Victor Herbert.

Suggestions for listening,
study and discussion

1.   Listen to Gilbert and Sullivan's *The Mikado*. Compare it to a European grand opera of the same period like Verdi's *Otello* or Wagner's *Die Meistersinger*. What makes it different? What are some similarities between them? What are some differences and similarities between grand opera, operetta, and a modern American musical?

2.   Additional European operettas you may profit from hearing are Offenbach's *The Tales of Hoffmann;* Johann Strauss's *Die Fledermaus;* and both *H.M.S. Pinafore* and *The Yeoman of the Guard* by Gilbert and Sullivan.

3.   Compare the musical style and lyric content of the Stephen Foster Minstrel Show song ("My Old Kentucky Home," "Camptown Races," "Old Folks at Home," etc.) with the style of music and lyrics in operetta, particularly Gilbert and Sullivan.

4.   The Mulligan shows made dramatic heros of the common man. How do musicals like *'West Side Story,' 'My Fair Lady,' 'Fiddler on the Roof,' 'Damn Yankees,'* and *'Porgy and Bess'* continue that theme?

B. THE AGE OF OPERETTA

Victor Herbert was born in 1859 and, having shown considerable gifts in music as a child, was educated in the manner of a classically trained artist. He was a graduate of the Stuttgart Conservatory and an accomplished 'cellist who played in the major orchestras of Europe and America under such greats as Brahms, Liszt, and Mahler. His wife was a noted soprano of New York's Metropolitan Opera, and for six years Herbert was the conductor of the Pittsburgh Symphony Orchestra.

Impressive as these credentials are, it was not in the realm of the classical concert hall that he was destined to achieve his greatest fame but rather in the lighter climate of the Broadway operetta. Influenced by the European imports of the 1880's Herbert turned his hand to operetta composition in the early 1890's with the work of *La Vivandiere,* written for the most glamourous songstress of the age, Lillian Russell. Unfortunately, Russell steadfastly refused to perform the work, claiming that Herbert was not well-known enough for a star of her stature. The production was never mounted, and the score was subsequently lost.

Had Russell known she was turning down a man destined to become the giant of his era, she might have thought twice. Indeed, the history of the American Musical Theatre fairly overflows with the misjudgments of people, many of whom were too filled with their own importance or too lacking in artistic ability to recognize works of quality. Whatever Russell's shortcomings, however, Victor Herbert knew his worth and persevered. In 1894 he produced the operetta *Prince Ananias.* Its success launched spectacular career.

Over the next thirty years, Herbert wrote an incredible number of works including undying classics like *Babes in Toyland* (1903), *The Red Mill* (1906), and *Naughty Marietta* (1910). In all, he wrote over fifty operettas and gave us such musical gems as "Toyland," "The March of the Toys," and "Ah, Sweet Mystery of Life."

In listening to Herbert's work today, it is important to bear in mind his strengths and the interaction of those strengths with the demands of operetta. Herbert's genius was not as a dramatist nor as an architectural composer in the mold of a Beethoven or Brahms. He was essentially a weaver of melodies who did not question the trite lyrics, stock plots, or dimensionless characters presented him by his librettists and lyricists. Indeed, such theatrical sophistications were not the point of the operetta genre.

In his book *The Story of America's Musical Theatre* (Philadelphia: Chilton, 1961. pp. 13-14), author David Ewen writes the following of operetta:

> It did not matter if the plot was...confused...if a song or dance had little or no relevance...that the characters were made from the same cardboard and papier-mache as the scenery. But what did matter—and matter a great deal—was that the scenes and costumes were nice to look at, the tunes delightful to listen to, and the performers pleasant

to watch. The senses had to be catered to, never
the intellect.

Herbert's compositional strengths were exactly suited to the nature of operetta, and in operetta, his weaknesses didn't matter. He continued to reign until the audiences tired of the formulas of grand froth, though his work never completely left the national consciousness. He died in 1924 as his popularity was on the wane, never to know that the new media of film and television would revive such classics as *Babes in Toyland* and catapult them to the level of national treasures.

As great a figure as Herbert was, however, it is important to know that he did not write in a vacuum or preside over an era solely by himself. The age of operetta produced other authors who were equally able to walk the path which Herbert trod. Franz Lehar's *Merry Widow* (1907), *The Pink Lady* by Harry Morton and Ivan Caryll (1911), and *Madame Sherry* (1910) by Karl Hoschna and Otto Harbach, for example, all enjoyed great popular success. But the two figures who most often rose to Herbert's level in the world of the operetta were Rudolph Friml and Sigmund Romberg.

Between 1910 and 1935 Friml turned out twenty operettas including *Rose Marie* (1924) and *The Vagabond King* (1925), both ranking in stature with anything by Victor Herbert. Among Friml's most famous songs were "Indian Love Call," "Only a Rose," and "Some Day," all of which are still performed in theatre and concert hall.

Romberg's best-known works included *Blossom Time* (1921), a rather historically inaccurate account of the life of Franz Schubert using many of Schubert's classic themes; *The Student Prince* (1924); *The New Moon* (1928), which included such song greats as "One Kiss," "Softly As in a Morning Sunrise," and "Lover, Come Back to Me"; and *The Desert Song* (1926) for which his librettist was a young man destined for greatness in the musical theatre, Oscar Hammerstein II.

By the time Romberg's career peaked, however, the operetta was a dying genre. Trite theatre, even if camouflaged by great melody, was no longer palatable in a society beset by monumental problems both at home and abroad. Depression, prohibition, and the rise of fascism were simply not conducive to the fluff and grandeur of the fairy tale stories which were the hallmark of the operetta. On the other hand, operetta was not a totally dead form. It would reappear from time to time in the decades ahead, often following the formula of *Blossom Time* in the use of classical music as an underlying unifying force. For example, in 1944 Robert Wright and George Forrest brought *'The Song of Norway'* to Broadway. It was, again, a romanticized portrayal of a classical composer—this time Edvard Grieg—using Grieg's own melodic themes. In 1953, the same team presented *'Kismet,'* a fanciful story of Arabian intrigue which employed the music of Russian composer Alexander Borodin. Twenty or so years after its initial run, *'Kismet'* would reemerge with an all-black cast headed by songstress Eartha Kitt in a retitled production called *'Timbuktu.'*

It is also important to know that the age of operetta did not contain operetta to the exclusion of other styles of musical theatre. The grandeur of Herbert, Friml, and Romberg may have dominated the years between 1895 and 1925, but there were other kinds of musicals and other great musical writers, some of whom produced works which would both artistically and financially outstrip anything from the world of operetta.

The influence of Victor Herbert notwithstanding, it is fair to say that from its inception until the Great Depression, the Minstrel Show also continued to exert a powerful force upon the American musical stage, not in its original form but in the burlesques, extravaganzas, and revues which it parented.

The comedy team of Weber and Fields, for example, starred in many popular musical satires around the turn of the century. Often, they incorporated great vaudeville stars into their burlesques as extra attractions. Lillian Russell, Fay Templeton, and Marie Dressler all appeared with them at one time or another. Occasionally, a burlesque production would even launch a new star into the theatrical heavens. Al Jolson, in fact, was one such example, and he would come to be the impetus for many of the extravaganzas of the era, using them to introduce such hits as "California Here I Come," "Toot-Toot-Tootsie," "Swanee," "April Showers," and "Rock-A-Bye Your Baby with a Dixie Melody."

The pure variety show nature of big burlesques and extravaganzas was so popular that many theatres, such as New York's Hippodrome, were constructed especially for them. Again and again, great stars and great producers filled the theatres with ever-new routines, ever-bigger and grander formats. None was more skilled at this kind of musical theatre than producer Florenz Ziegfeld whose *'Ziegfeld Follies'* became Broadway's biggest annual event. In one glittering, glamourous show after another, Ziegfeld produced twenty-one revues, giving the public stars like Nora Baynes, Fanny Brice, W.C. Fields, Eddie Cantor, Will Rogers, Sophie Tucker, Ed Wynn, and Al Jolson; and composers such as Irving Berlin writing songs like "A Pretty Girl Is Like a Melody."

From a purely historical point of view, the plotless, characterless nature of the extravaganza and revue would never produce any work of theatrical substance. Indeed, they were not designed to do so, and in those times when the lack of substance has haunted Broadway, the gala revue has always been brought out to fill the void. In the musical theatre of the 1980's, for example, in shows like *'42nd Street'* and *'My One and Only,'* we can clearly hear the echoes of eras past in the tap dances and production numbers of the present.

In the age of operetta, however, there were those whose heart was clearly neither in the fairy tale romances of Herbert nor the opulently vacuous productions of Zeigfeld. The most important such person was none other than "Mr. Broadway" himself, George M. Cohan. A product of the vaudeville circuit, Cohan had spent years as a variety show entertainer in a family act which included his parents and sister. He was thoroughly schooled in the styles of the revue and extravaganza, and when he finally emerged as a dynamic solo star, he incorporated the elements of his past with talents and musical formats uniquely his own.

Because the revue was so dramatically empty, Cohan insisted that his musicals have a coherent, if not profound, plot. Yet because he felt the fanciful plots of operetta to be alien to the experience of real people, he centered his story line about the common man—much as the Mulligan shows had done in generations past. Finally, because he was intensely patriotic, he found every excuse to insure that his characters were identifiably American and that everything American be glorified. A firm knowledge of the music and lyrics of vaudeville, heros made of common men, an intense nationalistic fervor, and his own electrifying stage personality—how could he miss? In 1904 with himself as composer, lyricist, librettist, director, producer, and star, he presented Broadway with *'Little Johnny Jones,'* the story of an American horse racing jockey. It was a smash, and he followed it up in 1906 with another, *'Forty-*

Five Minutes from Broadway.' For the next twenty years, he rode the crest of the wave he himself had created, a new brand of musical comedy which gave us song classics like "Give My Regards to Broadway," "You're a Grand Old Flag," and "Over There."

Even when his brand of musical began to fade in popularity, he remained a potent theatrical force. In 1933 he starred in Eugene O'Neill's *Ah Wilderness* and in 1937 came out of retirement to play the role of President Franklin Delano Roosevelt in the Rodgers and Hart satire *'I'd Rather Be Right.'* Indeed, Roosevelt cited him with a special award for the patriotism he had inspired through works like "You're a Grand Old Flag" and "Over There," and in 1942 he was immortalized in the film biography *Yankee Doodle Dandy,* for which actor James Cagney received universal critical acclaim.

If not for the profundity of his product, then certainly for his originality and individuality, Cohan stood as a contradistinction to the stodgy world of operetta and the dramatically void world of the revue. The force of his personality was a harbinger of the musical theatre to come, and the trend of which he was a part included some of the greatest names in Broadway history.

Watching Cohan in the years before 1920, learning from his brand of musical and applying to it their own individual talent were a host of young writers on whose shoulders the mantle of Broadway's future would fall—Jerome Kern, George Gershwin, and the team of Richard Rodgers and Lorenz Hart. Together they formed a musical stream for which Cohan served as wellspring.

Kern, for example, born in 1885, spent his early adult life writing for the pop music market in both New York and London. He, in fact, enjoyed some success with tunes like "They Didn't Believe Me." But more than just writing individual songs, he studied the new products of Cohan and from 1911 to 1925 began to experiment with his own kind of musical theatre. In particular, he formed an alliance with librettist Guy Bolton and lyricist P.G. Wodehouse, producing a series of intimate, low-budget shows for the three-hundred-seat Princess Theatre in New York. The "Princess Theatre Shows" were nothing like the flamboyant productions of Cohan, but they owed to Cohan a measure of their daring originality.

Gershwin, too, chose a distinctively original path. Starting as a Tin Pan Alley songster with tunes like "I'll Build a Stairway to Paradise" and "Somebody Loves Me," Gershwin devoted himself to serious classical training, fusing the compositional idioms of the concert hall with the harmonic, melodic, and rhythmic elements of jazz. The results were works of genius which would become legendary masterpieces of Americana—works like "Rhapsody in Bluc" and *'Porgy and Bess.'*

Rodgers and Hart came from the tutored environment of Columbia University in New York and spent their apprenticeship writing creative vignettes for the campus. Their first big professional break came in the mid-1920's when they wrote a series of revues known as the "Garrick Gaieties" which sported such hits as "Manhattan" and "Mountain Greenery." Their style was young, fresh, and quite separate from the formality of operetta and the extravaganzas of Ziegfeld. If not a carbon copy of Cohan, they were the results of his influence.

Until the operetta and extravaganza ran their course, none of the younger generation of musical composers would exert a dominating influence. By the mid-1920's, however, it was clear that Herbert and Romberg, Zeigfeld and Cohan were exhausting their separate audiences. Not just on Broadway, but socially and politically, the nation seemed poised on a new era. The Roaring Twenties, destined to collapse in a Great Depression, was no longer a fertile environment for theatrical progress.

Suggestions for listening,
study and discussion

1.   Listen to Victor Herbert's *Babes in Toyland*. What is his musical style? Compare it to that of his predecessors (like Stephen Foster) and successors (like Richard Rodgers). Describe and discuss the lyrics to his music. Compare them to those of pop songs of the post-World War II era.

2.   Listen to some of the music of the revue and extravaganza. There is an album which may be helpful in this regard: *Follies, Scandals, and Other Diversions*. It was made for the Recorded Anthology of American Music Series by New World Records. How does the revue style differ from operetta? Compare the vocal styles of singers like Fannie Brice with those in the Victor Herbert operettas.

3.   The films *The March of the Wooden Soldiers* (the Laurel and Hardy cinema remake of *Babes in Toyland*) and *Yankee Doodle Dandy* (the Cohan biography starring James Cagney, Walter Huston, and Joan Leslie) provide an excellent look at the musical theatre of the Age of Operetta. After viewing them, contrast Cohan's style with that of operetta. You may wish to discuss the award-winning performance of Cagney as well.

C. THE AGE OF DEVELOPMENT

The years between 1925 and 1945 were among the most turbulent in American history, indeed, in the history of all mankind. Global economic crisis and global warfare were such pervasive parts of living that they affected every facet of human endeavor. The theatre, always to some extent a mirror of its environment, was no exception. In the wake of bread lines and soup kitchens, the invasion of Ethiopia, and the Austrian Anschluss, the opulent froth of operetta and revue seemed out of place, perhaps even callous and cavalier. It was not that large-scale productions were compelled to disappear from the musical stage, although to some extent they did, but rather that they express some meaningful literary or social or philosophical point of view, something to unite them with the tenor of the times.

The change in the American Musical Theatre can be most clearly seen in the year 1927 when two productions impacted upon the Broadway scene as few have ever done before or since. They were *'A Connecticut Yankee'* and *'Show Boat.'*

Having properly apprenticed in the milieu of college and review, Richard Rodgers and Lorenz Hart decided to fuse their talents with those of American writer Mark Twain, adapting Twain's satire on the legend of King Arthur. It was not the last time the legend would be tapped as the source of a musical. Thirty-three years later, Lerner and Loewe would return to it once more for their production of *'Camelot.'* But in 1927, the use of great literature as the dramatic underpinning of a musical was far more daring. *'A Connecticut Yankee'* opened on November 3rd at New York's Vanderbilt Theatre to glowing reviews. Brooks Atkinson called it "novel...in the best of taste," and Alexander Woolcott delighted in the "fetching songs of Mr. Rodgers," songs like "Thou Swell" and "My Heart Stood Still." If nothing before it had, *'A Connecticut Yankee'* clearly established Rodgers and Hart as a major force on Broadway.

Strong as the impact of *'A Connecticut Yankee'* was, however, it was minor compared to that of *'Show Boat.'* The music was by Jerome Kern, the book and lyrics by Oscar Hammerstein II, the production an adaptation of Edna Ferber's novel *Show Boat*. To understand why *'Show Boat'* was so startling, it is necessary to know that the original book was not simply a colorful slice of life on the Mississippi. Rather, it was a significant social documentary which dealt with serious and profound themes— broken marriage, the role and treatment of women, interracial relationships, and the oppression of blacks. In fact, when Kern first asked Ferber for permission to adapt her novel for the musical stage, she refused him, believing that her material would be prostituted in the manner of the girly shows and revues of the past. It was only when Kern promised her a new kind of musical theatre that she relented.

Kern was true to his word, not only in his faithfulness to the intent of the novel, but even in the quality of his material and the way in which it was integrated with the libretto. Previously, most musicals had used a story or character as the excuse to plug a song, hype a star, or mount a production spectacular. In *'Show Boat,'* the situation was reversed. Song, lyric, dance, comedy all emanated from the characters themselves and the situations into which the plot forced them. It was truly unique. No formulas, no simulated earthquakes, no flapping chorus girls or prancing vaudeville stars—just poignant characters, a story of importance, and some of the most moving music and lyrics of all time ("Bill," "Why Do I Love You?," "Make Believe," "Can't Help Lovin' Dat Man," "Ol' Man River"). When the reviews came out, Brooks Atkinson wrote, "Mr. Kern and Mr. Hammerstein have discovered how musical plays, which used to be assembled, can now be written as organic works of art."

However, it was not enough that *'Show Boat'* was an artistic triumph. Its impact was also due to the fact that it was an enormous financial success. At first, very few people expected the venture to succeed, including Florenz Ziegfeld who financed the production with great misgivings. One friend after another urged the authors to abandon the project in favor of the tried and true styles of the past, but like great pioneers in any field, Kern and Hammerstein stuck to their guns, refusing to cower in the face of lesser talents. How right they were is demonstrated by the raw statistics of the show. The initial two-year run grossed $50,000 a week. A second run in 1932, which included the incomparable Paul Robeson in the role of Joe, ran for another 180 performances and generated the first record album devoted exclusively to the material of an original musical. There were several movie versions, a world tour, a 1946 revival which played over 400 performances, and countless millions of dollars from record and sheet music sales.

'Show Boat' stands not only as a milestone of the musical theatre but also as a message, and the message is this: there is never any comparable substitute for artistic quality nor any doubt that, properly showcased, works of quality sell and endure. That message would be delivered over and over in the years ahead. We will see it in the launching of *'Oklahoma!'* in 1943 and *'West Side Story'* in 1957; and there are many who wish it would be heeded again in the bleak musical days of the 1980's.

The echoes of 1927 resounded through the decade of the 1930's not only in the continuing partnership between Rodgers and Hart but particularly in the works of George Gershwin and the enigmatic Cole Porter.

Porter was an intellect, a sophisticate, a man of wealth and social standing who had been graduated from Yale with a kind of suave urbanity that would carve a very prominent niche for himself in both Broadway and Hollywood. His personal life was at once lavish and decadent, and he fused the positives and negatives of his character to create music and lyrics which were clever, witty, and at times profane with double meanings and sordid references. Songs like "Love for Sale," and "I Get a Kick Out of You" were filled with the veiled innuendo of topics like prostitution and drug addiction; but they were also hauntingly beautiful, enormously popular, and, to those who preferred not to look beneath the surface of the words, innocuously acceptable. If not for the profundity of *'Show Boat'* or literary substance of *'A Connecticut Yankee,'* then for an individual style which stood in diametric opposition to the grand operetta, Porter allowed the American musical to move into a new era of social grace and upper class charm. In 1928 he gave us *'Paris'* and the risque hit "Let's Do It;" in 1929 he wrote *'Fifty Million Frenchmen'* and the wonderful ballad "You Do Something to Me." Also from 1929 came *'Wake Up and Dream'* with its hit "What Is This Thing Called Love." The 1930's saw seven more productions including *'The New Yorkers,' 'The Gay Divorcee'* (which starred Fred Astaire and featured one of Porter's greatest tunes, "Night and Day"), and, perhaps his most famous show, *'Anything Goes'* (with hits like "You're the Top" and "I Get a Kick Out of You").

By contrast, George Gershwin was neither suave nor profane. His personality was that of a serious, studious artist, and his output for the musical theatre was hardly given over to the frivolity of the upper class. In 1930, with libretto by George S. Kaufman and Morrie Ryskind and lyrics by his brother, Ira, Gershwin composed *'Strike Up the Band,'* a satire on war. He followed it in 1931 with *'Of Thee I Sing,'* a biting commentary on American politics. Of this effort, the great critic George Jean Nathan wrote, "It is a landmark in American satiric musical comedy." It was, in fact, the first American musical to receive the Pulitzer Prize.

But neither *'Strike Up The Band* nor *'Of Thee I Sing'* would reach the artistic level or carry the tremendous impact of Gershwin's 1935 classic, *'Porgy and Bess.'* Technically, because its dialogue is musical recitative as opposed to speech, *'Porgy and Bess'* is almost always classified as an opera rather than a musical. However, Gershwin was clearly a composer who straddled two worlds, the popular one of Tin Pan Alley and the one of the concert hall. Whatever the classification of *'Porgy and Bess,'* the magnitude of its artistic achievement and the effect it had on the American Musical Theatre must be acknowledged.

The book was by DuBose Heyward; the lyrics by Heyward and Ira Gershwin; the story, a poignant drama about a crippled black man living amid the squalor of a ghetto called Catfish Row. There was nothing frivolous about the subject. It was a work of folk art which forced America to come face to face with its own racism and with the heroic proportions of black suffering. Yet, in the unfolding of the story, there was nothing trite or melodramatic about the plot. In the end, when Porgy decides to rise above his handicap and poverty to search for the woman he loves, it doesn't matter that he is black. He speaks for all of us; he embodies all mankind.

The music with which Gershwin unfolded his libretto was as dramatic, original, and artful as the story itself. Arias like "Bess, You Is My Woman Now," "I Loves You, Porgy," "It Ain't Necessarily So," and "Summertime" have risen far beyond the simple classification of Broadway hit. They are staples of all musical theatre, permanent and enduring in quality.

'Porgy and Bess' elevated the American product to the level of great art, and if many in the years ahead would not duplicate its accomplishments, then at least it would remain a standard against which other works might be measured, toward which other artists might aspire.

Now carried on the crest of the wave they themselves had helped to create, Rodgers and Hart produced works in which great literature and high art became a central force. For example, in 1936, they integrated the ballet "Slaughter on Tenth Avenue" into their musical, *'On Your Toes.'* It was choreographed by no less than the legendary George Balanchine and was a presaging of the work of Agnes de Mille in *'Oklahoma!'* and Jerome Robbins in *'West Side Story.'* Then in 1938, Rodgers and Hart wrote *'The Boys from Syracuse,'* an adaptation of Shakespeare's *The Comedy of Errors.* Again, their example would be imitated in later years with *'Kiss Me, Kate'* (the adaptation of *The Taming of the Shrew*) and *'West Side Story'* (based on *Romeo and Juliet*). Just as Verdi had reached out for classic literature in works like *Otello* for the operatic stage, the American musical was developing a taste for better things. Clearly, the loose fantasies of operetta and meaningless dramas of comedic revues were now things of the past. By the time Rodgers and Hart did their last great show *'Pal Joey'* in 1940, for which they adapted the short stories of John O'Hara, meaningful literature as the basis of a musical was no longer the exception but the rule.

Finally, the Age of Development was one in which the American musical acquired an awareness of social and political issues. To works like Gershwin's *'Strike Up the Band'* and *'Of Thee I Sing'* were added a host of others dealing with topics ranging from overt political satire to socialist unionism.

In 1932, for example, with a book by Moss Hart, Irving Berlin satirized both government and business in *'Face the Music.'* Harold Rome's 1937 revue *'Pins and Needles'* dealt with labor relations in the garment industry and was no doubt the inspiration for the Broadway hit *'The Pajama Game'* nearly twenty years later. But by far the two most celebrated authors of the social-comment musical were Marc Blitzstein and Kurt Weill.

Nineteen thirty-seven's *'The Cradle Will Rock'* by Blitzstein was perhaps the most celebrated work of its kind during the era. It espoused the causes of left wing unionists and was sponsored by President Roosevelt's Works Projects Administration to bring economic relief to unemployed actors. Produced by John Houseman, directed by Orson Wells, *'The Cradle Will Rock'* was itself the object of political turmoil. Right wing pressure was brought to bear which canceled the WPA's financial support of the show just hours before the curtain was to rise on opening night. In an almost unbelievable real life melodrama, a vacant nearby theatre was found, the audience moved into it, and the show performed sans scenery or costumes, with Blitzstein playing the orchestra parts from his piano score.

Magically, the wacky rendition proved to be a hit both artistically and financially. When a new producer was found and the show reopened in a fresh 1938 production, the setless, orchestraless, costumeless format was preserved—this time by choice.

Blitzstein was a serious, avant-garde, classically trained composer who had turned his hand to Broadway in the name of social awareness. It was no coincidence that much the same could be said of Kurt Weill.

Weill was a refugee from fascist Europe who had achieved a fair degree of fame there and who would duplicate the feat in America. His best-known works, *'The Threepenny Opera,' 'Mahagonny,'* and *'Knickerbocker Holiday'* were all, in one way or another, pointed political satires. At times the American audiences embraced Weill; at times they did not. *'Knickerbocker Holiday,'* for example, was fairly well-received. With Pulitzer prizewinner Maxwell Anderson as librettist and lyricist, and Walter Huston engaging in the role of Peter Stuyvesant, the show had a fairly substantial run and its most important ballad, "September Song," became a classic.

By contrast, *'Mahagonny'* did not do as well either in its original run or in any of its revivals. Even *'The Threepenny Opera,'* Weill's adaptation of John Gay's *The Beggar's Opera* of 1728, at first did not do well. Despite over four thousand European performances, its original 1933 New York debut was a failure. It was not until 1954 when Blitzstein composed a modernized version that the American audience accepted it. Running in an off-Broadway theatre, it enjoyed a six year life, had over two thousand performances, and made the song "Mack the Knife" an American hit.

Whatever the peaks and valleys of Weill's career, however, by the end of the decade of the 1930's, the American musical had lost its innocence. With the outbreak of World War II in 1940 and the death of Larry Hart in 1943, the American Musical

16. *The Age of Development*

Theatre again stood poised on the edge of a new era, the era of its greatest achievements.

Suggestions for listening,
study and discussion

1. Listen to *'Show Boat'* and compare its music and lyrics to those of Foster, Herbert, and Cohan.

2. Listen to *'Porgy and Bess.'* Compare its style to that of *'Show Boat.'* Would you consider it an opera or musical? Does the distinction matter to you? If so, why? If not, why not?

3. In what ways did the "Age of Development" affect the American musical? How do you feel about the trends of the 1930's? Do you think they advanced the musical art or robbed it of qualities which might better have been preserved?

4. As an adjunct to #3, what do you think should be the intent of a musical? If you were authoring one, what would you wish it to convey? How do the works of Kern, Gershwin, Porter, Weill, Blitzstein, and Rodgers and Hart compare with your ideal?

D. THE GOLDEN AGE

It would seem logical that the turmoil and terror of World War II would reduce the activities of Broadway to a trickle. In the midst of all the devastation and suffering, one could hardly expect musical theatre of epic or innovative proportions. Yet it was precisely at this time that a major event took place, the production of *'Oklahoma!.'*

The team which had produced *'Show Boat'* in 1927, Kern and Hammerstein, by 1942 was no longer together. In 1939 Kern had given up writing for Broadway in favor of a career composing for Hollywood movies. Hammerstein had fallen on lean times with a succession of failures both in New York and London.

The team which had produced *'A Connecticut Yankee'* in 1927, Rodgers and Hart, by 1942 was no longer together. Hart, always an "undisciplined worker" (to quote historian David Ewen), was in poor health and battling alcoholism. Rodgers had been left without a partner, and he had just received an interesting offer from New York's Theatre Guild to set Lynn Riggs's play, *Green Grow the Lilacs,* as a musical.

There was Hammerstein, alone and hungry to regain the successes of his past. There was Rodgers, alone and looking for a partner with whom he could do *Green Grow the Lilacs*. It was a marriage made in heaven. Not only would Rodgers and Hammerstein turn Riggs's play into *'Oklahoma!,'* they would go on to dominate the American Musical Theatre for the next twenty years, becoming the most prolific, successful, and artistically astute team in the history of the art.

From the inception of *'Oklahoma!,'* neither Rodgers nor Hammerstein was content to accept the formulas of the past. Riggs's play, dealing as it did with folk characters and folk themes, seemed to demand new approaches—just as the folk themes of *'Porgy and Bess'* had done. Later, Hammerstein would write of this phenomenon: "(We realized) that such a course was experimental, amounting almost to a breach of implied contract with a musical-comedy audience...(but) once we had made the decision, everything seemed to work right, and we had the inner confidence people feel when they have adopted the direct and honest approach to a problem."

The tried and true patterns of successful musicals were intimately known to both Rodgers and Hammerstein. They were, after all, seasoned veterans of the Broadway wars. The opening scene of Act I was traditionally a rousing chorus number designed to gain the attention of the audience and "hook" them into the story, as it were. The same general rule held for the last scene of Act I. "Give them something to remember during the cigars and cocktails of intermission," the idea went, "and they'll come back eager for Act II." "Keep the dancing snappy," another formula had it, "and stay away from long, boring ballets." "Don't interrupt your big songs with a lot of dialogue. People hate to lose the thread of a good melody." All this and more were well-known to Rodgers and Hammerstein, and all this would be discarded by them.

'Oklahoma!' opened with a lone character on stage and proceeded for a good deal

of the first scene with only three actors. Act I ended with an Agnes de Mille ballet of extensive proportions. Song and dialogue were interspersed even to the point where whole scenes were interpolated between the first statement of a melody and its conclusion. The villain of the drama was treated at times with comedy and, in one scene, was given a remarkable solo song which made the audience sympathetic to him. In a host of ways, *'Oklahoma!'* challenged the theatrical assumptions of the past and ushered in not only a new team but a new era.

Few but the authors had confidence in *'Oklahoma!'* when the money was being gathered for its production. The $83,000 needed to raise the curtain was obtained only with great difficulty. But from opening night in 1943 until Hammerstein's death in 1960, the judgments behind the show were vindicated hundreds of times over, and the Rodgers and Hammerstein partnership became both financially and artistically a musical dynasty.

'Oklahoma!' was followed by a cavalcade of hits: *Carousel* (1945), *Allegro* (1947), *South Pacific* (1949), *The King and I* (1951), *Me and Juliet* (1953), *Pipe Dream* (1955), *Flower Drum Song* (1958), and *The Sound of Music* (1959).

There was never anything trivial about a Rodgers and Hammerstein show. No matter what artistic level was achieved—and in efforts like *'Carousel,' 'South Pacific'* and *'The King and I,'* it was generally conceded to be the level of a musical classic— the authors made a conscious and consistent attempt to work with great literature and profound, universal, humanistic themes. *'Carousel,'* for example, an adaptation of Ferenc Molnar's *Liliom,* dealt poignantly with the power of redemptive love and the bonds between the living and the dead. *'South Pacific,'* based on James Michener's *Tales of the South Pacific,* presented audiences with the themes of bigotry, war, and the ultimate triumph of love over hate. In *'The King and I,'* the authors raised the issues of women's rights, international politics, and slavery. *'The Sound of Music'* dealt with fascism and the need for every soul to stand and be counted in times of crisis.

Rodgers and Hammerstein characters were rarely trite, their plots rarely predictable. For example, they were never slaves to the cliche of the "boy meets girl, boy loses girl, boy finds girl" storyline which pervades so many works of musical theatre. In *'Carousel,'* the hero dies and reappears in order to give his daughter the courage to live. In *'The King and I,'* Anna and the King of Siam develop one of the most moving relationships in all theatre without ever resorting to a sexual romance. Endings are not always happy; even villians are given dimensional characterization which make them more real and understandable.

The work of Rodgers and Hammerstein was inspirational to the American theatre. It encouraged a rash of "content musicals" the likes of which Broadway had never before seen. So many important works followed *'Oklahoma!,' 'Allegro,'* and *'Carousel'* that from 1946 to 1970, it really behooves one to study Broadway's musical highlights year by year. In the pages below, we will do just that.

1946. The gap between *'Carousel'* in 1945 and *'Allegro'* in 1947 was filled neatly by Irving Berlin's *'Annie Get Your Gun,'* the story of Annie Oakley which starred Ethel Merman and ran for over one thousand performances. If not the most profound offering of the era, it nonetheless became a staple of the repertoire with classic songs like "They Say It's Wonderful," "The Girl That I Marry," and "There's No Business Like Show Business." It is also of interest to note that the producers of *'Annie Get Your Gun'* were none other than Rodgers and Hammerstein.

1947. Besides *'Allegro,'* 1947 saw the birth of two musical classics: *'Finian's Rainbow'* by Burton Lane and E.Y. Harburg, and *'Brigadoon'* by a team destined for greatness, Alan Jay Lerner and Frederick Loewe.

'Finian's Rainbow' fused Irish fantasies of gold and leprechauns with the social issues of greed and racial prejudice. It gave us some memorable songs: "Old Devil Moon," "Look to the Rainbow," and the unforgettable "How Are Things in Glocca Morra?," to name just three.

'Brigadoon' was also a fantasy set in a magical town in the highlands of Scotland. It was important on several fronts. First, it launched Lerner and Loewe into the front rank of musical writers. Second, it was the first musical to receive the coveted Drama Critics Circle Award as best play of the year. Third, it added some new classics to the Broadway song repertoire, hits like "Come to Me, Bend to Me," "There But for You Go I," and "Almost Like Being in Love."

1948. Again, the gap between Rodgers and Hammerstein shows (*'Allegro'* in 1947 and *'South Pacific'* in 1949) was neatly filled by an intervening great, this time *'Kiss Me, Kate'* by Cole Porter. Writing both music and lyrics (as Cohan and Berlin had done before, and Jerry Herman, Frank Loesser, and Meredith Willson would do after), Porter drew upon Shakespeare's *The Taming of the Shrew* to compose song classics like "Wunderbar" and "Always True to You in My Fashion." *'Kiss Me, Kate'* drew rave reviews, won the "Toni" (Antoinette Perry) Award as the year's best musical and was one of a select handful of shows to run for over one thousand performances.

1949. Besides *'South Pacific,'* which is generally considered one of the greatest musicals of all time, 1949 also saw a Kurt Weill production entitled *'Lost in the Stars.'* In keeping with his own training and development (referred to earlier), Weill produced a work of deep social content. Based on Alan Paton's *Cry, the Beloved Country*, the story dealt with race prejudice, love, and death in South Africa. The nature of the vocal and choral writing has often led people to consider *'Lost in the Stars'* an opera. Critic Olin Downes was quite firm in this categorization, and indeed the revival of the work took place at the New York City Opera. Not many of the show's songs were hits in the popular sense of the word, though the title song, "Lost in the Stars," was recorded by Frank Sinatra, among other artists. However, with a fine libretto by playwrite Maxwell Anderson, *'Lost in the Stars'* continued the trend that musicals of the "Golden Age" aspire toward excellence.

1950. 1950 saw the propulsion of Frank Loesser to the forefront of American musical composers with the hit show *'Guys and Dolls.'* It was actually his second musical, the first being the 1948 production of *'Where's Charley?,'* which itself ran for over seven hundred performances. *'Guys and Dolls'* continued the tradition of adapting good literature to the musical stage by using as its basis the short stories of Damon Runyon. It ran for twelve hundred performances and gave us such hits as "If I Were a Bell," "I've Never Been in Love Before," and "A Bushel and a Peck." Critic John Chapman called it the best musical of the year. He was not alone. It won the "Toni," Drama Critics Circle, and Donaldson Awards for 1950.

20. The Golden Age

1951. *'Paint Your Wagon'* by Lerner and Loewe was the only show of substance in 1951 to rival the Rodgers and Hammerstein production of *'The King and I,'* and it is not generally held in the same esteem. It was neither a critical nor financial success and ran for less than a year. Its chief contribution was the fact that it continued the collaboration of Lerner and Loewe, and that, as we shall see, was a most fortunate thing. By contrast, *'The King and I,'* with Yul Brynner and Gertrude Lawrence in the lead roles, took Broadway by storm. It was immediately recognized as a great musical and in over thirty-five years of revivals (most with Brynner in the role of the King) it never lost its importance. It is a must for any student of the American Musical Theatre to study and, hopefully, perform.

1952. 1952 was not a banner year for Broadway. The highlight of the year, in fact, was not a musical but a revue entitled *'New Faces of 1952.'* It was written by a variety of people and had as its aim the introduction of new talent. Both Eartha Kitt and Paul Lynde came to prominence as a result of it. The 1952 show was part of a *'New Faces'* series which had appeared in 1934 and 1936 and would surface again in 1956. The revues were small, creative productions more in the mold of the old Princess Theatre Shows than the Ziegfeld Follies. They were evidence that the format which had grown out of the olio of the minstrel show was still a viable one, and in the years following 1970, when content musicals declined precipitously, the format would be revived yet again.

1953. Things picked up in 1953 with the appearance of four musicals. Besides Rodgers and Hammerstein's *'Me and Juliet,'* there was Cole Porter's *'Can-Can,'* an operetta called *'Kismet,'* and a show entitled *'Wonderful Town'* whose composer, Leonard Bernstein, was to become one of the most important conductor/composers of the century.

Though each show possessed a certain individual charm, and each rose to a certain level of achievement, none was destined for greatness. None would be compared to efforts like *'Oklahoma!'* or *'The King and I.'* *'Kismet'* was an adaptation by Robert Wright and George Forrest of the music of Alexander Borodin, the Russian romanticist of the nineteenth century. Its fanciful Arabian setting and convoluted plot were colorful if not profound. *'Wonderful Town'* (music by Bernstein, lyrics by the team of Betty Comden and Adolph Green) was based on the novel, *My Sister Eileen,* dealing with the exploits of an Ohio lass in New York's Greenwich Village. Compared to some of Bernstein's other work— *'Candide,'* *'West Side Story,'* The Jeremiah Symphony, The Chichester Psalms, or the incidental music for *On the Waterfront*— *'Wonderful Town'* was not his best effort. With a book by Abe Burrows (whose work on *'Guys and Dolls'* had made him a major Broadway librettist), *'Can-Can'* fared better than the rest. Hits songs like "C'est Magnifique" and "I Love Paris" made the rather frivolous plot palatable, and the show ran for almost nine hundred performances. *'Me and Juliet'* was not in the same league with the rest of Rodgers and Hammerstein. It was a return to musical comedy whose only memorable song was "No Other Love." It was not well-received by the critics (Walter Kerr calling it "tongue-tied" and "disconnected") and it ran not even a year.

Rather than being a profound year, 1953 seemed only to keep the promise of musical greatness alive.

1954. The promise bore a bit more fruit in 1954 with the production of *'Fanny'* and *'The Pajama Game.'*

Marcel Pagnol's plays about waterfront loves in Marseille served as the basis for *'Fanny.'* The libretto by S.N. Behrman and director Joshua Logan managed to capture much of Pagnol's style. The music and lyrics of Harold Rome did not produce any hits beyond the title song but served the story admirably. The show ran for almost nine hundred performances with the great Metropolitan Opera star Ezio Pinza in the role of Cesar. Pinza had taken Broadway by storm as Emile de Becque in *'South Pacific.'* He now returned for his last musical. He died in 1957.

'The Pajama Game' by Richard Adler and Jerry Ross was a lighthearted return to the themes of unionism which had so engulfed the 1930's. Now, however, there was nothing left wing about union-management disputes nor anything controversial about the union leader girl falling in love with the management guy. *'The Pajama Game'* was one of the few musicals to make it past one thousand performances with hits like "Hey, There," "Steam Heat," and "Hernando's Hideaway."

1955. By far, the best show of the 1955 season was the Adler-Ross follow-up to *'The Pajama Game,'* a modern day setting of the Faust legend entitled *'Damn Yankees.'* It was the perennial story of the man who sells his soul to the devil in exchange for youth—this time the youth and talent of a major-league baseball player intent upon defeating the New York Yankees. The musical ran for over a thousand performances, won the "Toni" Award, and gave us the hit songs "Whatever Lola Wants," "Two Lost Souls," and 'You've Got To Have Heart." Unfortunately, it was the last Adler-Ross show. Jerry Ross died in 1955 at the age of thirty, the victim of a chronic lung infection.

None of the other shows of 1955—the Rodgers and Hammerstein production of *'Pipe Dream,'* *'Plain and Fancy'* by Arnold Horwitt and Albert Hague, or even *'Silk Stockings'* by Cole Porter—compared to *'Damn Yankees.'* None drew critical acclaim or achieved great financial success.

1956. By any reckoning, 1956 was one of the greatest years in the history of Broadway, producing such works as *'L'il Abner,'* *'Bells Are Ringing,'* *'Mr. Wonderful,'* *'Most Happy Fella,'* *'Candide,'* and *'My Fair Lady.'*

'Most Happy Fella' by Frank Loesser was an adaptation of Sidney Howard's *They Knew What They Wanted* and incorporated the hits "Joey, Joey, Joey," "Big D," and "Standing on the Corner." *'L'il Abner'* (lyrics by Johnny Mercer, music by Gene de Paul) was based on Al Capp's cartoon characters. It was not a critical success despite almost seven hundred performances and the hit ballad, "Namely You." *'Mr. Wonderful'* by Larry Holofcener, George Weiss, and Jerry Bock was the weakest musical of the year, chiefly because its plot was merely a contrivance to showcase the talents of performer Sammy Davis, Jr. It did give us the hit songs "Mr. Wonderful" and "Too Close for Comfort," however. By comparison, *'Bells Are Ringing'* was a much stronger effort. Lyrics by Comden and Green, music by Jule Styne, the show ran for nearly a thousand performances and included "The Party's Over" which became a classic pop ballad.

None of these shows, good as some of them were, however, could hold a candle to the two masterpieces which appeared with them in 1956, *'Candide'* and *'My Fair*

Lady.'

'*Candide*' was based on the great social satire of the same name by Voltaire. The libretto was by Lillian Hellman, one of America's most celebrated playwrights. Lyrics were by Richard Wilbur; music by Leonard Bernstein. The talent behind the show was as impressive as anything Broadway had mustered, yet the production was a dismal failure, running for only a scant seventy-three performances. Critically, it received contradictory reviews. Brooks Atkinson declared that Voltaire's "eighteenth century philosophical tale (was) not ideal material for a theatre show," yet Robert Coleman declared that "it towers head and shoulders above most of the song-and-dancers you'll get this or any other season."

Part of the problem with '*Candide*' was that its style was misunderstood; part of the problem was that it was vastly ahead of its time and needed a more astute mounting to realize its potential. To appreciate these statements one must know that '*Candide*' is "story theatre," that is, a style of theatre which is not a representation of reality but rather one in which a narrator speaks to the audience as if the audience were listening to a bedtime fable. Such a genre allows fact and fantasy to intermingle, and it is a perfect vehicle for the philosophical archetypes of Voltaire's novel. The story theatre genre was new to Broadway. Perhaps people did not know how to respond to it, but like any stylization, it cannot be viewed with the expectations of realism, just as a fairy tale cannot be judged by the standards of a non-fiction biography.

Given the theatrical style of '*Candide,*' Bernstein's score fit it to a tee, for what Bernstein wrote was not the popularizations of Broadway tunes but a twentieth century spoof of eighteenth century opera. From the point of view of craftmanship, the arias, rhythms, use of counterpoint, choral scoring, and orchestration in '*Candide*' were simply so far beyond the banal talents of Broadway that, to Broadway patrons, they were unrecognizable.

The vindication of '*Candide*' took twenty years to accomplish. Two revivals, one in the mid-1970's, the other in the early 1980's, established the show as a classic comic opera satire. The first revival, staged by producer/director Hal Prince, ran over seven hundred performances. It was set in the round with multiple playing areas and imaginative effects which dazzled the critics. The second revival was done by the New York City Opera.

By comparison, '*My Fair Lady,*' the other great production of 1956, was an immediately recognized classic. The musical was an adaptation of George Bernard Shaw's *Pygmalion* and as such dealt with the depth of social themes, irrascible humor, and superb characterizations which had made Shaw one of the greatest playwrights of all time. The music and lyrics of Lerner and Loewe were perfect expressions of the book and certainly their finest work, surpassing even '*Brigadoon.*' The production was brilliantly staged and directed by the legendary Moss Hart. Finally, the performances by Rex Harrison as Professor Higgins and Julie Andrews as Liza Doolittle were hailed as being among the greatest in the history of the American musical.

Every critic everywhere was unequivocal in proclaiming '*My Fair Lady*' the musical of the year—indeed, of many years. It won the "Toni" and Drama Critics Circle Awards, grossed untold millions of dollars, ran for well over two thousand performances, enjoyed many world tours and revivals, and gave us one great musical number after another ("The Rain in Spain," "Get Me to the Church on Time,"

"On the Street Where You Live," "I've Grown Accustomed to Her Face," "I Could Have Danced All Night," "With a Little Bit of Luck," and more).

For the sheer elegance of its craftmanship—of which we shall speak later on—if not for the profundity of its theme and magic of its entertainment, *'My Fair Lady'* made 1956 a year to remember in the history of the art.

1957. It is difficult to imagine the level of 1956 being duplicated in another year, but so it was in 1957, if not in the quantity of material, then surely in the quality of it, for in 1957 both *'West Side Story'* and *'The Music Man'* came to Broadway.

Based on Shakespeare's *Romeo and Juliet, 'West Side Story'* was set in the Hell's Kitchen slums of Manhattan with the Montagues and Capulets now personified by warring street gangs. The stark violence and bigotry of New York were depicted with a kind of brutal poetry by the libretto of Arthur Laurents, the lyrics of Stephen Sondheim, and the music of Leonard Bernstein. The staging and ballet of Jerome Robbins were integrated with the kind of surrealistic set which Arthur Miller had used so effectively in *Death of a Salesman.*

But the real magic of *'West Side Story'* was contained in the level of craftmanship exhibited by each creative artist involved. The story, of course, had long since been regarded as one of the greatest in literary history. To it, Laurents added believable dialogue and dimensional modern characterizations. Sondheim's lyrics were at once profound, profane, and poetic. Bernstein's gifts as a classically trained composer had always elevated him above the mediocrity of Tin Pan Alley, but now he soared to new heights of melodic motion, harmonic ingenuity, and rhythmic vitality. In works like "Tonight," "Maria," "One Hand, One Heart," "Somewhere," "America," and "I Feel Pretty," the American musical rose once more to the level of great art.

Producers Robert Griffith and Harold Prince—at first fearful that the audiences of Broadway, used to lesser diets, might not support a quality product—were vindicated in their judgment. *'West Side Story'* was unanimously acclaimed as a masterpiece. It ran over seven hundred performances, returned after an absence of only a year to run for another two hundred and fifty, was revived on Broadway and at Lincoln Center several times, and was turned into one of the most financially and artistically successful movies of all time. Like *'Show Boat,' 'Porgy and Bess,'* and *'Oklahoma!'* before it, *'West Side Story'* reiterated the message that quality pays dividends.

'The Music Man' with book, lyrics, and music all by Meredith Willson was in spirit and content diametrically different from *'West Side Story.'* It was upbeat, traditional in format and musical style, and set not amid the squalor of a modern slum but in the wholesome turn-of-the-century town of River City, Iowa. But in terms of the quality of its craftsmanship, it was equally deserving of praise. Brilliant patter-song lyrics, a marvelously integrated melodic fabric, clever dialogue, and a story so honestly engaging that its triteness became charming—all this and a great performance by Robert Preston as music man/con artist Harold Hill made the show an instant hit. It brought us tunes like "Seventy-Six Trombones," "Till There Was You," and "Goodnight, My Someone" and ran for well over thirteen hundred performances, winning both the "Toni" and Drama Critics Awards even over *'West Side Story.'* Between both shows, it was another unforgettable year for the American Musical Theatre.

1958. The highlight of 1958 was another Rodgers and Hammerstein show, *'Flower Drum Song.'* It was an innocent comedy set in the Chinese Quarter of San Francisco, and although it was critically well-received, it did not advance the development of the art as *'Oklahoma!,'* *'South Pacific,'* and *'The King and I'* had done. The hit song from the production was "I Enjoy Being a Girl." After a run of less than two years, *'Flower Drum Song'* was taken on tour and eventually to Hollywood where a movie version was made.

1959. Once again the "Golden Age" poured its riches onto the streets of Broadway. 1959 gave us three musical gems: *'The Sound of Music,'* *'Fiorello,'* and *'Gypsy.'*

In their last show, Rodgers and Hammerstein adapted the story of *The Trapp Family Singers* to create *'The Sound of Music,'* a touching if sentimental account of love amid the growing specter of fascism in pre-World War II Austria. Some critics dismissed the show as overly emotional, but most recognized the level of its craftsmanship and gave it glowing reviews. Certainly, the public loved it. With songs like "Climb Every Mountain," "Do Re Me," "Favorite Things," "Sixteen Going on Seventeen," and "Edelweis," it ran for over fourteen hundred performances. The movie version became one of the biggest box office hits of all time, and in the quarter century following its birth, it became a national treasure much as Herbert's *'Babes in Toyland'* had done.

Oscar Hammerstein died during the run of *'The Sound of Music.'* On August 23, 1960 he succumbed to cancer at his home in the hills of Pennsylvania. Without him, Rodgers would never again achieve the heights of greatness. His passing not only marked the end of a theatrical genius but the beginning of the end of the "Golden Age." Though great musicals would continue to be written for a decade, the giant who had fired Broadway's development from *'Show Boat'* to *'Oklahoma!'* would not be replaced.

'Fiorello' with lyrics by Sheldon Harnick and music by Jerry Bock was the most decorated show of the year, winning the Pulitzer Prize, Drama Critics Award, and "Toni" Award for best musical. It was based on the life of New York City Mayor Fiorello LaGuardia, and in the manner of the politically-inspired shows of the 1930's combined first-rate entertainment with pointed social satire.

The third gem of 1959 was a musical about the theatre itself. *'Gypsy'* (music by Jule Styne, lyrics by Stephen Sondheim) was based on the autobiography of stripper Gypsy Rose Lee. At first glance, one might expect a bawdy production in which Broadway glamourizes itself with a kind of narcissistic revue. Many musicals of both stage and screen had, in fact, done just that. From shows like *'Annie Get Your Gun'* to movies like "The Seven Little Foys," America had always been bombarded by theatre folk telling us how great theatre folk are. And why not? What could be more expected—the egomaniacal world of the performer with the loudspeaker of mass media at its fingertips? Even the award systems, the "Toni's" and "Oscar's" and "Emmy's," had always been the theatre's way of patting itself on the back, glorifying its own and hyping new business.

'Gypsy,' however, avoided all that, for in essence it was not really about the theatre but about the art and agony of child-rearing. True, it tells of a "stage mother" who pushes her children to the point where they and she become neurotic shells of what they might have been, but the theatre is only incidental to the theme. In *'Gypsy,'*

we face the universality of a Western family structure which believes it owns its children and therefore has the right to determine the course of their lives. It is the story of emotional child abuse, of the disgrace of parents who try to overcome their own failures by living through their kids. It is the real tragedy behind the ubiquitous American dream of having "my son become a doctor."

Not just for wonderful songs like "Small World" and "Everything's Coming Up Roses," but for a skilled and poignant look at the way in which families destroy themselves, *'Gypsy'* earned a place as one of America's premier musicals.

1960. 1960 was another banner year for Broadway. *'Tenderloin,' 'Wildcat,'* and *'The Unsinkable Molly Brown'* were but the unheralded curtain-raisers for what was to come. The real stars were *'Bye, Bye, Birdie,' 'Camelot,' 'Oliver,'* and *'The Fantasticks.'*

'Bye, Bye, Birdie' by Charles Strouse and Lee Adams was a fun-loving spoof of adolescent behavior based on the hysteria which followed Elvis Presley's induction into the Army. It was greeted by the critics as pleasant satire and ran for just over six hundred performances. *'Camelot,'* following on the heels of *'Brigadoon'* and *'My Fair Lady,'* was the third hit for the team of Lerner and Loewe. However, the critics were bound to compare it with *'My Fair Lady,'* and by comparison it was flawed. A text which lacked cohesion, a mixture of scenes which were never really humorous on the one hand and never consistently poignant on the other, left the critics with, as Richard Watts put it, "modified rapture." However, the production did run for over eight hundred performances and went on to become a spectacular Hollywood movie.

'Oliver' (music and lyrics by British composer Lionel Bart) was an adaptation of Charles Dickens's novel. With songs like "Consider Yourself" and "As Long As He Needs Me," it managed to capture the blend of social pathos and comedic characterization which had long since made Dickens one of the great novelists of all time. But even more, *'Oliver'* ushered in an era of English influence. Its success sparked other imports from Great Britain which complemented America's homegrown successes for the next two decades. Thanks to *'Oliver,'* Broadway was now becoming something of an international arena for musical theatre.

By far, the most unusual show of the year—perhaps of any year—was *'The Fantasticks.'* Nothing about it fit the mold of a Broadway musical. To begin with, strictly speaking, it wasn't a Broadway show. It ran, rather, in a small off-Broadway theatre with a seating capacity of barely three hundred, the Sullivan Street Playhouse. Next, it had a cast of only eight characters, one of whom was a mute. It used no set save a rope, a blanket, and some scraps of furniture. Its props were almost non-existent, and it was scored for nothing more than a piano and harp. Yet in its simplicity was elegance; in its naivete, wisdom.

The book and lyrics were by Tom Jones, the music by Harvey Schmidt, two newcomers from Texas. They based their work on a play called *Les Romantiques* (The Romancers) by Edmond Rostand, the author of the classic *Cyrano de Bergerac*. Rostand's play was an allegory on the relationship between children and their parents, particularly that phase of childhood where adolescents mature, fall in love, break the bonds of home, and discover the world for themselves. He unfolded his universal plot using the device of archetype characters and a story theatre narrator with a touch of poetry and whimsy. Schmidt and Jones wisely decided not to tamper with a master. Their narrator, El Gallo, spins his tale around two fathers and their love-struck children with the grace of a fine painter. What *'Candide'* had done on a grander scale, that is, the use of non-representational theatre as a setting for philosophical allegory, *'The Fantasticks'* now did with a small cast in the intimacy of an off-Broadway house.

The critics were dumbstruck, their reviews contradictory at best. But producer Lorenzo Noto had faith in his show and kept it running week after week despite substantial losses. Gradually, the public itself began to become fascinated with the fantasy and simple beauty of the show. Houses started to fill and even the critics took a second, more considered look.

After a quarter of a century, *'The Fantasticks'* was still running at the Sullivan Street Playhouse, the longest-running off-Broadway show in the history of the American theatre (perhaps any theatre). It is an acknowledged masterpiece with songs like "Soon It's Gonna Rain" and "Try To Remember" and a style of presentation decades ahead of its time. Not coincidentally, it rewarded its producer and backers with a return on their original investment of well over five thousand percent, proving again that quality and courage are an unbeatable combination in the world of the musical.

1961. 1961 was not a busy year for Broadway. Its most notable achievement was the return of the partnership which had created *'Guys and Dolls'* ten years earlier: Frank Loesser writing music and lyrics, Abe Burrows (and others) doing the book. The new show was *'How To Succeed in Business Without Really Trying,'* a satire on the American morality and immorality of getting ahead. It received rave reviews, won every major award of the year, and ran for over fourteen hundred performances (to that time, the sixth longest-running production in Broadway history). Chief among its contributions was the fact that it used the vehicle of story theatre once again with great effect. J. Pierpont Finch, the main character (played admirably by Robert Morse), periodically addressed the audience, sharing with them the secrets of his successful climb from window-washer to Board Chairman. As it had done with the philosophical satire of *'Candide'* and *'The Fantasticks,'* the device proved irresistibly theatrical in *'How To Succeed...'*

The second noteworthy event of 1961 was another British import, *'Stop the World—I Want To Get Off'* by newcomers Anthony Newley and Leslie Bricusse. It continued the trend which had begun with *'Oliver'* to make Broadway an international arena of musical theatre.

1962. The major event of 1962 was the emergence of Stephen Sondheim as both composer and lyricist of his own shows. The man who had given Broadway the outstanding lyrics of *'West Side Story'* and *'Gypsy'* now joined the likes of Loesser, Porter, and Willson with *'A Funny Thing Happened on the Way to the Forum.'* *'Forum,'* as it was called, was a comedic satire of love and social morality set in ancient Rome. In spirit, it was very much a throw-back to the bawdy burlesques of the early 1900's. Plot and character were less significant than gag and innuendo, and indeed they were meant to be. For what it was, an unpretentious evening's entertainment, *'Forum'* pleased both audience and critic alike.

Of perhaps more importance than the show itself was—of all things—the length of its title. In *'Forum...,' 'Stop The World...,'* and *'How To Succeed...,'* it was becoming "trendy" to put shows with long titles on Broadway and even more trendy to refer to them by their shortened nicknames. In and of itself, the trend of titling productions was not significant. What was significant, however, was the growing use of trends themselves.

In the absence of individually creative shows, new material, or anything substantive to say, from the mid-1960's on, Broadway would take to imitation as the most convenient road to critical or financial success. What was a trend of titles in the early sixties would develop later into trends of racial casting, sexual exhibitionism, and theatrical content. In the wake of the social conscience-raising of Dr. Martin Luther King, for example, Broadway began to turn out "black cast shows." The black *'Hello, Dolly!,' 'Purlie,' 'The Wiz,' 'Your Arm's Too Short To Box With God,'* and *'Sugar Babies'* all sought to capitalize on racial overtones. The religious revivalism and born-again Christianism of the 1970's and 1980's would lead to shows like *'Godspell'* and *'Jesus Christ, Superstar.'* The gay rights movement of the 1980's would bring shows like *'La Cage Aux Follies'* to Broadway. The reemergence of the revue format after 1970 would give us *'Eubie,' 'Ain't Misbehavin','* and a host of others. The post-1970 penchant for dance would be exploited in *'A Chorus Line,' 'On Your Toes,' 'My One and Only,' '42nd Street,'* and more.

To some extent it is natural, even desirable, for a nation's theatre to reflect its current history and social movements. Certainly, Broadway had seen such things in abundance during the 1930's. However, trendism is more than social reflection. It is theatrical exploitation, the stifling of individually creative efforts in favor of formula-writing which seeks not to advance the development of theatre but merely to capitalize on what is momentarily popular. As we shall see, trendism was a major factor in the decline of the American musical after 1970.

1963.   The highlight of 1963 was an intimate production by the composers of *'Fiorello,'* Harnick and Bock, entitled *'She Loves Me.'* It was based on the Miklos Laszlo play *Parfumerie* which had twice been made into a Hollywood move (*The Shop around the Corner* and *In the Good Old Summertime*). If not profound, at least *'She Loves Me'* had charm, and above all it continued the association of Harnick and Bock which in the next year would give Broadway a work of pure brilliance.

1964.   1964 was another magical year for the American musical theatre. Besides *'Fade Out-Fade In,' 'What Makes Sammy Run,' 'High Spirits,'* and *'Golden Boy,'* three shows of first-rate quality were produced: *'Hello, Dolly!,' 'Funny Girl,'* and *'Fiddler on the Roof.'*

'Hello, Dolly!' (book by Michael Stewart, music and lyrics by Jerry Herman) was a rousing, fun-loving musical based on Thornton Wilder's play *The Matchmaker.* It was neither innovative nor profound but possessed all of the ingredients of a spectacular evening's entertainment. Critics found it flawed yet loved its ebullience. Howard Taubman of the New York Times wrote, "...Mr. Stewart's book has settled for some dull and cheap lines...but (the show has) qualities of freshness that are rare..." Richard Watts added, "...the fact that it seems to me short on charm, warmth, and the intangible quality of distinction in no way alters my conviction that it will be an enormous success." If Watts was implying that the American audience could be

seduced into substituting theatrical hoopla for dramatic content, he was absolutely correct. *'Hello, Dolly!'* ran for well over a thousand performances and became something of a classic.

'Funny Girl,' which also ran for over a thousand performances, was another of Broadway's narcissistic efforts. Music by Jule Styne (of *'Gypsy'* fame), lyrics by Bob Merrill, *'Funny Girl'* was based on the ill-fated romance between the great Fanny Brice and gangster Nick Arnstein. The show was not long on social content, but it was poignant nonetheless and provided a vehicle for newcomer Barbra Streisand which catapulted her to stardom. If for nothing else, Streisand's rendition of ''People'' made *'Funny Girl'* worth the watching.

By far, however, the best thing of 1964 was Harnick and Bock's *'Fiddler on the Roof.'* In an unforgettable performance as Tevye, the Jewish milkman of Anatevka, Zero Mostel brought the short stories of Yiddish writer Sholom Aleichem to life in a blend of comedy and tragedy which Broadway had not experienced since *'West Side Story.'* Story theatre, ethnic humor, historical documentary, and social commentary mingled with music and lyrics of unsurpassing craftsmanship to make *'Fiddler'* one of the masterpieces of all time. ''Sunrise, Sunset,'' ''If I Were a Rich Man,'' ''Matchmaker,'' ''Tradition,'' ''Now I Have Everything,'' ''Far from the Home I Love,'' ''Miracle of Miracles,'' ''To Life,'' and ''Anatevka'' provided an unending stream of laughter and tears. Joseph Stein's book not only made the suffering of the Jewish people in Czarist Russia real, it made the plight of all oppressed people a universal theme which the American melting pot could not ignore. *'Fiddler'* became a national treasure. It captured every award in sight, became to that point in time the longest-running musical in Broadway history, and grossed untold millions in profit for its investors.

1965. By comparison with 1964, 1965 did not produce as much, though two of its shows, *'The Roar of the Greasepaint—The Smell of the Crowd'* and *'Man of La Mancha'* did command attention. *'GreasePaint'* by Newley and Bricusse continued the trend of British imports and long titles. *'Man of La Mancha'* by Mitchell Lee and Joe Darion continued the trend of using great literature as the underpinning of a production, adapting as it did Cervantes's classic *Don Quixote* for the musical stage. Of the two, *'La Mancha'* was by far the more important show, winning both ''Toni'' and Drama Critics Awards for 1965 and giving us the heroic ballad, ''The Impossible Dream.'' With raves from the critics, *'La Mancha'* joined the select thousand-or-more performance circle.

1966. 1966 was the last great year of the ''Golden Age,'' producing, among others, four musicals of substantial quality: *'The Apple Tree,'* *'Cabaret,'* *'Mame,'* and *'I Do! I Do!.'*

'The Apple Tree' was quite a change of pace for Harnick and Bock after *'Fiddler on the Roof.'* It was in actuality a collection of three one-act musicals based on Mark Twain's *The Diary of Adam and Eve,* Frank Stockton's *The Lady and the Tiger,* and Jules Feiffer's *Passionella.* It was an inventive experiment by an already established team.

'Cabaret' by John Kander and Fred Ebb was both critically and financially a hit. Running for over eleven hundred performances, it integrated the cabaret style

of Kurt Weill's pre-World War II Europe with the large-scale Broadway genre. It also integrated the variety numbers of the Kit Kat Club with a plot which unfolded personal drama against the fearsome panoply of Hitler's rise to power. It was, by all accounts, one of the strongest shows of the era.

'Mame' was Jerry Herman's follow-up to 'Hello, Dolly!' and was very similar in both spirit and content. Based on Patrick Dennis's novel *Auntie Mame*, it was a surefire audience-pleaser which ran for over fifteen hundred performances.

Finally, in 'I Do! I Do!' the imaginative team of Jones and Schmidt which had given us 'The Fantasticks' proved that their first success was no accident. In a moving setting of Jan de Hartog's *The Fourposter*, 'I Do! I Do!' traced the history of a marriage with humor and tenderness. It had only two characters (the husband and wife) and one set (their four-poster bed), but it was captivating and charming nonetheless.

1967-1970. From 1966 onward, the "Golden Age" wound down a scattering of noteworthy shows, none of which possessed either the genius or the impact of masterpieces like 'West Side Story,' 'My Fair Lady,' or 'Fiddler on the Roof.' Among those one could mention are 'You're a Good Man, Charlie Brown,' the 1967 production by Clark Gesner which was based on Charles Schultz's cartoon *Peanuts*; 'Hair,' the 1968 hippy revue by Galt MacDermot, Gerome Ragni, and James Rado; 1969's 'Seventeen Seventy-Six' (1776), the musical account of the birth of the Declaration of Independence by Sherman Edwards; Stephen Sondheim's 'Company' in 1970; and 'Purlie' by Peter Udell and Gary Geld, the 1970 adaptation of a 1961 Ossie Davis play about bigotry and racial prejudice in the American South.

The unbelievable explosion of the American Musical Theatre from 'Oklahoma!' in 1943 to 'Cabaret' in 1966 was over, and sadly, Broadway would now begin an era of decline which has lasted to the time of this writing. Just why the decline took place is a matter of some speculation, but in our last section on the history of the American musical we will explore some possible explanations. For now, it remains for us to investigate a few topics for study, listening, and discussion which will make the "Golden Age" more alive.

Suggestions for listening, study and discussion

1. Ideally, a student of the musical theatre should know every show mentioned in this brief history. Studying the librettos and scores of the repertoire is indispensable to the development of a performer. However, from a practical point of view it may be impossible to get a hold of every libretto and score—or even every record album. In the interest of some selectivity, therefore, the following dozen musicals of the "Golden Age" are recommended for in-depth viewing. Other shows might be chosen, but few would argue that the choices below do not deserve your time: *'Oklahoma!,' *'South Pacific,' *'The King and I,' *'Brigadoon,' 'Candide,' *'My Fair Lady,' *'The Music Man,' *'West Side Story,' *'Gypsy,' 'The Fantasticks,' *'Fiddler on the Roof,' and *'Cabaret.' (* indicates that these are available on film.)

2. Read through the libretto of Act I, Scene 1 of 'Oklahoma!.' How are dialogue

and song distributed? Does the distribution inhibit or aid the effect of the scene? Now try performing the scene. How does the distribution feel?

3. Read through Act I, Scene 1 of *'South Pacific.'* Compare it to the first scene of *'Oklahoma!.'* How many musical numbers are in the first scene of *'South Pacific?'* Notice how they are integrated with the dialogue and plot. With what does the scene begin and end? Did you find this device in your study of *'Oklahoma!?'* What do you think it contributes? Why do you think the authors used it?

4. How would you describe the King's song, "A Puzzlement," in *'The King and I?'* Compare it to the patter songs of *'The Mikado'* and Higgins's songs in *'My Fair Lady.'* How did the finale of *'The King and I'* affect you? How did you react to the "Little House of Uncle Thomas" ballet? Compare it to the dream ballet at the end of Act I of *'Oklahoma!.'*

5. Compare the representational style of *'Brigadoon'* to the story theatre allegory of *'Candide.'* How do they affect characterization and plot development? Does the musical style of each show fit its dramatic nature? Why or why not?

6. Pick a character in each of the musicals below and read one of his or her major speeches. Why did you choose the character and speech you did? What relevance have they to the central themes of the shows? *'My Fair Lady,'* *'The Music Man,'* *'West Side Story,'* *'Gypsy.'*

7. *'The Fantasticks,'* *'Fiddler on the Roof,'* and *'Cabaret'* all have narrators of sorts (El Gallo, Tevye, and the Emcee). Choose a speech and/or song from each show and perform it as the character involved. In what ways are the characters similar? In what ways are they different? Does the device of story theatre help or hurt you as a performer? What does it do to or for the musical as a whole?

E. YEARS OF DECLINE

Lehman Engel spent over forty years in the American Musical Theatre as a conductor, composer, and mentor. He was the recipient of three "Toni" Awards and the conductor of such productions as *'Fanny,' 'Call Me Mister,' 'Take Me Along,' 'Wonderful Town,'* and *'Brigadoon.'* In the mid-1960's, under the auspices of the performing rights agency Broadcast Music, Incorporated, he started a school for new young talent interested in learning how to write for the musical stage. From the inception of his workshop until his death in the early 1980's, Engel proved to be as gifted an educator as he was a conductor. He wrote two very important books on musical theatre, and it is worth noting his opinion regarding the state of the art after 1970. The following quote is taken from his text, *The American Musical Theatre* (New York: MacMillan, p.220). It was written in 1975.

> Surely we have progressed further along in time. Surely it is abundantly clear to everyone that shows like *'Henry Sweet Henry,' 'Minnie's Boys,' 'Jimmy,' 'George M.,' 'Coco,'... 'Zorba,'...* and many more like these—with their impossibly bad books and music that is supposed to make us nostalgic—are not indeed the progeny of *'Carousel,' 'West Side Story,'* and *'Fiddler on the Roof'*...By burning the bridges of our heritage...we will never build something worthily new...Today experimentation is so disorderly and unconnected that most of those who pride themselves on being a part of it are surely not going anywhere. They seize on popular trends, often achieve fame and fortune for a brief time, know nothing to begin with and end up really giving out nothing.

Seven years after Engel wrote that, on Sunday, November 14, 1982 to be exact, a column appeared in the New York Times. It was by Times critic Frank Rich, and it was entitled "What Ails Today's Broadway Musical?" The excerpt below is from his article.

> It seems like only a faint memory now but there was actually a time when it was a joyous experience to go to a Broadway musical...Those pleasures have pretty much vanished in recent years. The most durable American theatrical commodity...has lost so much fizz that we've lived to see the once unimaginable day when a British musical (like) *'Cats'* can steal Broadway's thunder...The great

31.

> promise of the serious musical has
> atrophied…(and) the proliferation of such poor
> shows wouldn't be so troubling a prospect if the
> serious Broadway musical were in healthy shape.
> If we could believe that a new *'West Side Story'*
> or *'Fiddler on the Roof'* were waiting in the wings,
> it might be easier to tolerate an onslaught of video-
> arcade extravaganzas.

What Engel saw in 1975 and Rich echoed in 1982 was seen and said by many other observers of the Broadway scene. The musical of social content, of character development and profound theme, was no longer to be found in the abundance in which it had once flourished. Replaced by the revival, the revue, the technological extravaganza, some wondered if it could be found at all. Rather than moving forward, Broadway regressed to its past, reinventing its history, producing works of mediocrity which contained the same flaws that productions had contained fifty, sixty, seventy years before.

There were, of course, some exceptions: *'Shenandoah'* (by Geld and Udell) and *'A Chorus Line'* (by Marvin Hamlisch and Edward Kleban) in 1975; *'Annie'* (by Charles Strouse and Martin Charnin) in 1977; *'Sweeney Todd'* (by Sondheim) and *'Evita'* (by Andrew Lloyd Webber and Tom Rice) in 1979. Even these, however, were not on the level of the great shows of the past. For many it was not to be argued whether or not Broadway had, in fact, declined. The arguments were, rather, why it had declined and what might be done to effect some sort of Renaissance. Such arguments are often speculative. They are many times beyond proof, subjective, and riddled with personal opinion and limited perspective. But that doesn't mean that they are necessarily false. In the space below, they will be stated, and it will be up to you, the reader, to debate them and decide what about them is wise and to be heeded, and what about them is folly.

The passing of great writers.   It seems obvious to say it, but the mere fact that many of the great musical theatre writers died, retired, or turned to other pursuits was enough to diminish the output of Broadway. By 1985, Hammerstein and Rodgers, Willson, Porter, and many other giants of the past lay in their graves. Still others like Lerner and Loewe were in full or semi-retirement. Those like Bernstein (who left his post as director of the New York Philharmonic and now spent most of his life conducting in Vienna) found different things to occupy their time and talent. One does not easily replace people of such stature. The glut of great musical writers active during the "Golden Age" was something unusual. That they would grow old and leave a void in the wake of their passing was something of an inevitability.

The lack of a training ground.   One of the things that had contributed to the large number of first-rate composers and lyricists was the tremendous activity generated by Tin Pan Alley (the region of New York City which housed most of the better music publishing companies of America). After the Second World War, Tin Pan Alley lost its preeminence as the capital of popular music. Hollywood films, the television industry, the world of commercial advertisement, and the new popular trends of rock 'n roll, soul, and country-and-western music each usurped a measure of talent which in olden days would have been directed to the musical stage. The B.M.I. workshop of Lehman Engel did aspire to replenish Broadway's dwindling stock of top-flight writers, but it was simply not enough to overcome the lures of Nashville, Detroit, Sunset Boulevard, and Madison Avenue. Nor did many colleges and music conservatories feel the calling. Rather than offering courses in the musical theatre, they seemed to be dominated by a penchant for the avant-garde, for training composers bent more on studio experimentation than theatrical communication. With the attrition of older talent and a failure to provide fertile training grounds for newcomers, Broadway was bound to suffer.

Economic pressure.   No society can escape the fiscal realities which dominate any given era, and from the mid-1960's onward, those realities were rather stark for America. The war in Vietnam was a tremendous monetary drain. The government borrowed; inflation soared. The rise of prices sparked a militancy among American unions to fight for commensurate wage increases, and the result was the worst economy since the Great Depression. Industrial growth slowed to a trickle while prices continued to climb. The cost of producing a musical escalated beyond control. The cost of a theatre ticket flew beyond the capability of the average man. In such an environment, producers were far more reluctant to invest the millions it takes to mount a musical production—especially when better than nine of ten new shows are destined to flop. Small wonder that the star-oriented revue and the revival of surefire warhorses seemed more attractive than chance speculations on a new musical.

The decline of education.   For an enormous variety of reasons (a change in social values, the increase in divorce rates, an overabundance of narcotics, the negative influences of television, war and political unrest, undisciplined educational experimentation, to name a few), America's schools experienced a precipitous decline between 1965 and 1985. Reading and writing levels dropped, SAT scores plummeted, classroom violence rose. By the late 1970's the level of the Broadway audience had changed. Adults who as children had been weaned more on TV situation comedies than classical literature were neither as willing nor as able to appreciate the content musical as generations past had been. It is, after all, difficult to accept filet mignon when your body is used to French fries and a coke.

Political shock.   The assassinations of John Kennedy, Robert Kennedy, Martin Luther King, Jr., and Malcolm X; the massive unrest and dissension over the Vietnam War; the sensationalism of Watergate; and the resignation of President Nixon created one of the most politically turbulent eras in American history. People felt numbed by it all to the point where the surest solace was escape into the nonage of things noncontroversial. As in the Roaring Twenties, "forget your troubles, come on, get happy" was a far more palatable way to deal with leisure time than watching philosophically provocative theatre. It is hard to accept the dead bodies of Tony and Riff in *'West Side Story'* when presidents and great leaders, young men and women on a combat field also lie in their graves. The generation less capable of appreciating profound theatre was also less inclined by the circumstances of the times to seek it.

Changes of culture.   When *'Oklahoma!,'* *'Brigadoon,'* *'My Fair Lady,'* and *'The*

Music Man' were first produced, women wore brassieres. Young girls in high school did not, as a rule, have sexual intercourse. Cocaine was practically unavailable. Hair styles were neat, clothing conservative, the elderly—at least on the surface—respected. Classrooms were orderly; the streets and subways of most cities relatively clean, relatively safe. By 1970 the morality and behavior of America and much of the Western world had changed radically. Sexual overtness, casual drug and alcohol use, family disintegration, criminal violence, an almost axiomatic suspicion of authority—all this was commonplace. Whereas before the messages and images of River City, Iowa were desirable to the theatre-goer, now the freakish body paint of *'Hair,'* the social anomie of *'Company,'* the cultural defiance of *'Grease'* were more in vogue. To the extent that people wish their theatre to reflect and approve of what they are themselves, audiences do not seek out or support shows whose values challenge them. One can argue that the American musical lost its content in part because the American culture lost its.

Changes of political style.   One of the things which presidents do is set a tone for a nation. Certainly, American presidents have a long history of doing that. With Franklin Roosevelt, Harry Truman, Dwight Eisenhower, and John Kennedy, the tone was of a very high level. FDR's rhetoric was inspiring to a nation beset by the Depression and global conflict. Truman's resolve and open honesty in World War II and Korea were an element of predictability and strength. Eisenhower was a war hero of enormous proportions. Kennedy was for many the Lancelot of a new age, inspired and inspiring. *'Camelot'* was, in fact, his favorite show, and when he quoted others, he quoted Aristotle and Robert Frost. By comparison, the turmoil of Vietnam tainted Lyndon Johnson. His style was not the classic style of Kennedy but a more vulgar one. He picked his dog up by the ears and was fond of showing the newsreel cameras the surgery scars on his belly. Richard Nixon, after all was said and done, was a disgraced, discredited president. Gerald Ford never commanded enough support to win election. Jimmy Carter was perceived not as an urbane sophisticate but an ineffectual country boy. Ronald Reagan quoted not Aristotle and Frost but Clint Eastwood's Dirty Harry. The presidents after Kennedy did little to inspire theatrical profundity. It was thus not part of the national gestalt, at least to the extent it once had been. In such circumstances, musicals like *'My Fair Lady'* seem far less in touch with the times than works like *'The Best Little Whorehouse in Texas.'*

The passing of great critics.   Finally, in the absence of social, educational, and political standards, it is all the more necessary that the theatrical critic be astute, intellectually honest, and willing to educate the theatre-going public. Sadly, one can argue that the great critics of the past were not replaced with people of similar calibre, at least not often. Consider what Broadway once had: George Jean Nathan, Alexander Woolcott, Brooks Atkinson, Walter Kerr, John Chapman, Olin Downes—people who were legendary in the history of criticism; people for whom Broadway even named its theatres. When they died or retired, they were, like the Broadway writers themselves, not easily replaced. Nor did the role of the critic remain what it had been. Where once the emphasis was on review with an eye toward training the public as to the good and bad in theatre, after 1970 it seemed to shift toward commercial hype designed more to bolster a sagging theatrical economy than to instruct or enlighten.

Indeed, in some quarters it was rumored that big critics were part of big business—paid off to keep certain theatres filled by slanting reviews to glorify the mediocre.

Put all these factors and forces together and it is not difficult to see why the American Musical Theatre fell from grace. The real question at this point in its history is: having fallen, having assessed the reasons for its fall, what can it do—what is it willing to do—to regain its former posture?

Suggestions for listening,
study and discussion

1.   One of the longest-running shows of the post-1970 era was *'Grease.'* Compare its music and lyrics to some of the shows of the ''Golden Age.'' Compare them to the music and lyrics of *'Annie,'* another post-1970 production.

2.   Research the quotes by Engel and Rich above. Try to read Engel's book and Rich's article. React to them. Do you agree or disagree with them?

3.   Invite your own local critic to address your class, or if possible visit him or her personally. With the critic as a guide, discuss the issues raised in the ''Years of Decline'' section of your text. Do they agree or disagree with the views expressed there? Ask them where they think the American Musical Theatre is now and where it is or ought to be going. Compare the answers of the critics to your own opinions on the subject.

PART II

The Elements of Production

A. PRELIMINARY PLANNING

A musical production begins long before auditions are held, long before crews are chosen or the first yard of muslin is tacked to the first flat. Sometimes performers forget this, simply because as a rule they are not involved in the preliminary planning of a show. Yet it is in the planning stage that most if not all of the truly critical decisions are made, decisions which somewhere down the road will spell either success or disaster for cast, crew, and pit. Selecting a show, assembling a production staff, planning a budget, modifying or arranging material, choosing a performance location, making techical plans, and establishing a production calendar are the essential elements of the preliminary process. It pays to be aware of them, of what goes into them, and particularly of how they effect the course of opening night.

Selecting a show. Whether one is writing a new show or producing an old one, deciding on the nature of the material is often the most critical step of the creative process simply because the nature of the material governs the demands ultimately placed upon producer, investor, director, audience, and performer. The wise selection of material takes into account the following elements: financial resources, availability of cast, availability of staff, and theatrical point of view. Let us look at each factor a bit more closely.

Mounting a musical production is a large economic undertaking. If it is an original production with a glamorous set and star-studded cast aimed at a Broadway audience, the bill can easily run several million dollars. Even if it is only the three-performance offering of a high school theatre club, it is apt to cost thousands. Knowing the financial resources available is critical to selecting the proper material since finances determine the scope and size of a production. Obviously, a well-endowed budget can result in a production of grand proportions. A more limited one would be better applied to something like *'The Fantasticks'* as opposed to *'Camelot.'* Later in this unit we will investigate the details of a budget, and you will have a chance to budget a hypothetical show of your own.

Beyond considerations of finance—though allied to them—are those of casting. In whatever environment a production is mounted (school, community, professional, etc.) and however a cast is finally chosen (by invitation, open audition, or a combination of processes), the producer must be certain he has the personnel necessary to fill all the roles. Common sense dictates that one doesn't do *'Seventeen Seventy-Six)* (1776)—a musical with a predominantly male cast—at a women's college, or try to produce a show like *'A Funny Thing Happened on the Way to the Forum'*—with its sophisticated humor and bawdy innuendo—at a junior high school. While smart producers try not to precast before auditions are held, they must nonetheless be confident that they can successfully cover parts from the talent pool available to them. Sometimes that is a fine line to tred.

Just as one must know there is cast enough for a production, one must know that there is staff enough. Later we will see in more detail what goes into choosing a production staff. For now, we need only be aware that an intelligent selection of material takes into account the directorial resources available. In the absence of a scintillating choreographer, for example, one does not produce *'Oklahoma!'* or, for that matter, write an original musical which calls for extensive and intricate dancing.

Finally, one mounts a show to express a certain theatrical point of view, to effect a certain kind of aesthetic communication. Composers, lyricists, librettists all write for many reasons. What they are greatly determines what they write. A desire to capitalize on a current trend, for example, may result in the exposition of certain subject matter, perhaps even govern the way in which the subject is presented. The desire to expose a certain philosophical theme, espouse a certain political view, encourage a certain financial return, experiment with certain ideas or technologies—all these will color the nature of any original material or the selection of any particular musical which is chosen for revival.

No theatrical viewpoint in and of itself determines the quality of a production. Material selected or written for purely fiscal reasons, for example, may still be first-rate in terms of craftsmanship. Commercialism of heart need not be synonymous with baseness of product. Nor, on the other hand, does a lofty theatrical ideal guarantee an artistically fine effort. Quality, as we shall see, is determined more by how the material is handled than by what it is or what lay in the hearts of its writers or producers. However, what it is in large part reflects what its authors wished to say, and what it says greatly determines the demands it makes upon those who perform and view it.

Assembling a production staff.   A musical is one of the most complex theatrical undertakings possible, drawing as it does on a wide diversity of art forms. Dance, drama, music, theatrical technology must all maintain their separate integrities at the same time they weave together to form an organic unity. The special nature of each component requires separate directors skilled in their individual areas. The integration of elements requires a kind of cooperation in which individual egos must eventually be sublimated to the well-being of the entire show. Assembling a directorial staff capable of doing all that is not an easy thing.

Generally speaking, musicals require at least the following staff members: a producer, a director for drama, a director for music, a technical director, a director for wardrobe and make-up, and a choreographic director. In some cases, individuals may wear more than one hat. The producer may also direct the drama; the musical director may also choreograph. However the labor is distributed, each directorial area must be covered, and one person must be endowed with the power to make final decisions when conflicting opinions arise. To understand the directorial staff as a whole, we will look at each member of it in a bit more detail.

The role of the producer divides itself into two essential areas: securing the financial resources needed and selecting the key directorial personnel. Once these two goals are accomplished, the producer becomes the conduit through which all production activities are coordinated. He pays the bills; rents the theatres; attends to legal matters; takes care of publicity and promotion; sees to it that tickets are printed, ushers are hired, schedules are met, popcorn is available for intermission. For all things business, he is the last word. In some instances, he may also have the final say in matters of casting. In rare instances, he may even have jurisdiction over artistic decisions.

The actual duties of a producer depend greatly on the type of production and the environment in which it occurs. Consider finances, for example. If the producer is mounting an original production which he hopes to bring to Broadway, his first job will be to secure the money he estimates it will take. This is generally done by forming limited partnerships with investors who think the production is a worthwhile risk. Such investors may be businessmen, theatre owners, publishers, private citizens, corporations, even the performers or authors themselves. Often a producer in this situation will finance out of his own pocket a so-called "showcase" performance of the musical. Such a performance usually consists of a reading of the work by paid professionals done without scenery, costumes, or theatrical technology (lights, microphones, props, etc.). A showcase production can be done at a small theatre. Sometimes it is even done in a rented hall at which potential investors—there by invitation—are "softened up" with a pre-performance cocktail party. On occasion, a professional producer may even dispense with limited partnerships and finance the entire operation himself. In recent years, the enormous cost of doing a musical has made this a rare occurrence.

The financial activites of producers in a professional environment are not at all the same as those of, say, school or college producers. Here, the musical is generally not an original one but rather a local remounting of a former hit with the production budget provided annually by the school itself. In such a situation, the producer must obtain permission to do the show from a performing rights agency which is charged with safeguarding the legal and financial aspects of it. Almost every well-known musical is registered with one of the following: Tams-Witmark, Music Theatre International, or The Rodgers and Hammerstein Library. These companies will send out contracts and collect royalties for the performance of a given show. They will also provide scripts and scores of the shows they handle—materials which are not available anywhere except through rental from the agency. How much the agency charges will depend upon the type of school, number of performances, seating capacity of the theatre, and the show itself. In such an environment, the financial activities of the producer are radically different from those encountered in an original Broadway effort, and in a similar way, the environment will govern the producer's activities in non-financial matters as well.

The drama director is responsible for most of the on-stage creative decisions. He supervises the audition process and selection of the cast. He is the chief architect of the staging, blocking, pacing, line delivery and characterization of the production. Generally, his is the last word in situations calling for aesthetic compromise. He must integrate the dramatic, musical, choreographic, and technical elements of the production to form a convincing whole. To the extent he is well-versed in areas beyond drama, to the extent his judgments are keen, to that extent alone the production will succeed. A poor artistic effort is generally his fault, if not because his own work is shoddy, then because he has failed to see and correct the shoddiness of others. In general, the tasks of the drama director are confined to one person. In opulent productions, however, with special problems and a large budget, those tasks may be distributed to directorial underlings. A director of dialogue, a director of staging and blocking, for example, are not unknown in a musical. If directorial assignments are scattered among several people, then the dramatic director has the added responsibility of coordinating them.

Theoretically, a musical director is responsible for training the voices, rehearsing the orchestra, and conducting the show from the pit on opening night. Most productions, however, divide the labor between at least two people: a vocal director, and a conductor who trains the instrumentalists and handles the pit during performances. It is rare to find one person competent enough for both jobs, and that is why good productions require the utmost teamwork and cooperation between the musical directors. Agreements on tempi, dynamics, phrasing, etc., must be worked out long before the curtain goes up. If they are not, the poor singer will be in for a very rough evening.

The tech director may be responsible for a host of things: lighting, sound, set design, set construction, set decoration, props, scene changes, curtains, etc. Generally, however, each area is given over to a specialist with one person acting as a coordinator and overseer. Even then, technical chiefs do their work in conjunction with other directors. The person who sets and later runs the lights, for example, is usually not the one who has designed the lighting plots. Lighting plots are mostly the province of the drama director. He works them out based on scenic designs and staging requirements and then gives them over to a technician for actual implementation. Again, the integration and coordination of directors in a musical production are intricate and require a great deal of teamwork. If one is planning a production, it is best to divide technical responsibilities among at least three people: an electrical expert to handle lights and sound; an expert in construction and decoration to design, erect, and paint the set; and a backstage expert to organize scenic, prop, and curtain crews.

The trappings of the body—wardrobe and make-up—are sometimes the responsibility of a single director who, with the drama and musical directors, will design and secure costumes (by purchase or personal sewing). In professional productions, the wardrobe and make-up responsibilities are often divided between experts in each area. Then, too, many actors prefer to do their own make-up.

The choreographic director is responsible for designing all movements done to music, be they strict dance, choreographed song, or the troop movements of big chorus production numbers. The choreographer must also teach the routines to the cast. This work has to be carefully coordinated with drama and music directors, and it is often accomplished with helpers like dance captains and staging experts who are supervised by a head choreographer.

A word here about directorial gender. The descriptions above use the word "he" merely as a literary convenience. Any of the directors in a modern production are just as likely to be women as men. Traditionally, wardrobe and choreographic jobs always admitted women. In recent years, with the advent of women's rights movements, more of the off-stage aspects of musical theatre have been handled by female directors. The important thing in assembling a production staff is not the gender of the people but the degree of expertise and—above all—the cooperation they bring to their tasks.

Planning a budget.   It would be impossible to list all the details of a production budget here simply because they vary so much from one production environment to another. It is very possible, however, to list the general categories common to most shows so that in planning your own production you have some sort of fiscal guideline.

The first expense one encounters is the fee to the authors of the show. If the production is a revival of an old show, the fee will manifest itself as a royalty/rental payment. If it is an original show, it may be a direct commission or a contractual arrangement for a certain percentage of the proceeds.

The next expense is for the people who put the production together. Directorial staff, arrangers, on-stage performers, pit musicians, crews, ushers, parking attendants, secretaries, and miscellaneous assistants must all be accounted for in a complete budget.

The house itself is often a major production expense. Rental fees for the theatre, utility bills, custodians, even concession stands which sell candy and soda during intermission must all be figured into the financial equation.

Advertising and publicity costs vary considerably from production to production, but most shows encounter something in this area. Printing, newspaper space, media commercials, and billboard signs are the more common items in an advertising budget. High-powered, well-financed productions may even retain advertising agencies and marketing personnel as part of the production staff.

If the production is a traveling one—a touring company or an original show which has trial runs out of town before the actual Broadway opening—then the cost of transportation, food, lodging, and even insurance must be added to the budget.

Finally, there are the direct costs of the musical itself: the wood, fabric, paint, and hardware to build and decorate the set; the labor and materials (or rental fees) for costumes; the cost of props, make-up, programs, tickets, and any lighting or sound equipment which does not come with the theatre. Again, these all vary with the nature and scope of the show.

Modifying or arranging material. Not so much in the launching of a new show but often in the production of a revival, material has to be modified. The reasons can be many: fresh locations, different casts, unworkable publications, constraints of budget, limitations of performers, to name a few. Consider the following examples.

The script of *'Guys and Dolls'* is loaded with specific staging directions: walk left, cross right, exit here, enter there. These directions were written for the original Broadway production, for that theatre, for that set. It is foolish to think that they could be transplanted literally to a fresh location, and indeed trying to do so might lead to a poor performance. It would have been intelligent if the librettists and publishers who produced the script had removed the extraneous staging instructions, but since they did not, the modifications must be made by the directorial and performing staff of the revival.

Now let us suppose that this revival is not a new Broadway mounting but the offering of a junior high school drama club. The differences in the capability of the cast and pit between the original professional production and the junior high version would be enormous, to say the least. A director would have to be nothing short of lunatic to expect a ninth-grade violinist to play or a ninth-grade soprano to sing exactly what occurred on opening night in 1950. Without compromising the integrity, order, or meaning of the material, orchestra parts would have to be simplified, keys would have to be changed to adapt professional level material to school personnel.

When Mary Martin opened in *'The Sound of Music,'* she was a star of many years standing, and from a vocal point of view, the years had taken their toll, forcing her singing range to that of a low alto. The part she played, Maria Rainer, a postulant about to enter the order of the nuns of Nonnberg Abbey, was really more suited to the lighter, more youthfully feminine range of a soprano. But Martin was a star with oodles of confidence and oodles of money behind her, so on she went as an alto—and she was just wonderful in the part. However—and it is a big however—when the score of the show was published, all of Maria's music was printed in the keys in which Mary Martin had sung. This was an unbelievable act of stupidity on the part of both publisher and authors because it forced every other Maria for all posterity to be a low alto. The only way out of this dilemma is, of course, to rearrange the music—which, by the way, is exactly what happened when soprano Julie Andrews was contracted to do the movie version of the show. If you are doing *'The Sound of Music'* and your Maria is a soprano, it will be your only way out as well.

'Candide' was not a success when it first opened in 1956, not so much because the content of the show was flawed but because the setting in which it was produced failed to show off its greatness. Eighteen years later, when producer/director Hal Prince revived the musical, it was hailed by the critics and enjoyed a healthy Broadway run. The reversal of fortune was due largely to the fact that the new *'Candide'* appeared in a completely different, highly imaginative setting. Prince rebuilt an entire Broadway theatre for his production, converting the normal proscenium configuration to a kind of theatrical football stadium reminiscent of the ancient Greek amphitheatres. Playing areas were not only those of the "grid iron" with seats tiered above it, but platforms built on every level of the "grandstand" at all points around the theatre. Characters walked and talked and even crawled amid the spectators who had to turn now this way, now that way, to follow the action. When a forest was called for, green craypaper showered down through the audience, making them a part of the set. Beds turned into boats with movable scenery parts, and even the orchestra was scattered into five locations, following the conductor on a video monitor. The entire effect was perfectly suited to the philosophical story theatre fantasy of the show. It was also perfectly expensive. Rarely does one have the money, much less the talent, to rebuild a theatre for a show. And so, to a large extent, material modification becomes a function of budget.

The stories of *'Guys and Dolls,'* *'The Sound of Music,'* and *'Candide'* above do not represent all of the reasons that material is—or should be—rearranged. They do, however, illustrate the why's and wherefore's of the technique, and it is a foolish producer or director who does not consider it with each new production.

Choosing a location and making technical plans. Once a budget has been determined, the selection of a location for a musical production is considerably easier than it otherwise might be. In fact, for productions like school shows, summer stock musicals, and many road shows, the theatre is a predetermined item which governs much of the budget. The high school musical, for example, doesn't enjoy the luxury of location selection. It is performed in the same auditorium with the same stage facilities and seating capacity year after year.

If choosing between several locations is a possibility, however, there are several important things to consider: size of stage, technical equipment available, seating capacity, accessibility to transportation, parking facilities, quality of acoustics, safety of building structure, adequacy of fire protection, etc. All of these will have a direct bearing on how many tickets can be sold, how many sets can be erected, how much publicity may be needed, etc.

Obviously, it is premature to make technical plans before knowing the hall in which a production will be mounted. The lighting plots, sound systems, and set designs are intricately bound to the configurations of the location involved. Once the location is known, however, these facets of a show are generally worked out well in advance. They may, of course, be modified during rehearsals, but the general blueprints can and should be assembled as part of the preliminary planning. If the show is a road show which will travel from location to location, the technical accoutrements of the production have to be simple, portable, and flexible so that they can fit a variety of halls. That, too, requires preliminary planning—perhaps a good deal more than if the production were confined to one location alone.

Establishing a production calendar. When all the other aspects of planning have been done, the directorial staff of a well-run production establishes a calendar giving deadlines for each phase of operations right up to opening night. The intelligence with which the calendar is set is critical, for once tickets are sold and publicity released, it is very difficult to change an opening night date. In the next section of your reading, we will discuss the elements of a production calendar in detail.

Suggested activity

In the theatrical environment in which you find yourself right now (school, community, professional, etc.), go through the preliminary planning for a musical production of your own. Select a show. Discuss how you plan to staff and cast it. Draw up an itemized budget. Choose a location. Design a set and draw up plans for lights and sound.

When you have finished, choose a second environment and compare the preliminary plans between the two. What has changed and why?

B. THE PRODUCTION CALENDAR

Once the basic planning for a production has been completed, it is time to begin the audition and rehearsal process itself. Keeping this process on track requires a schedule of events sometimes known as the production calendar. A good calendar is figured backward from the date of opening night and provides some leeway here and there for unforeseen emergencies like illness, equipment breakdown, severe weather, etc. Since productions vary so greatly one from another, it would be impossible to reproduce a calendar which would satisfy all conditions. The items below, however, are fairly common to most productions, and a discussion of them should at least provide a general background for any specific effort.

Auditions and crew selection.   The audition process should begin far enough in advance of opening night to allow cast, crew, and staff time to complete their assigned tasks to a point of excellence. How many weeks or months that is depends entirely upon the situation. A school production generally requires about ten weeks. Professional productions may take as much as a year.

Unless the cast is entirely known beforehand—a situation occurring only with repertory theatre or productions which employ a casting agency—auditions are usually preceded by some sort of advertisement "sending out the call," as it were, to the talent pool available.

Auditions may be "open" or "closed." An open audition is one in which all the participants (would-be cast members as well as staff) are present. Closed auditions are those in which only one actor appears at a time. There are positives and negatives to both methods. Closed auditions provide privacy but prohibit interaction between auditioners. Open auditions allow for interaction but may promote greater degrees of anxiety and imitation. Some auditions use both techniques. A basic cast is chosen via the closed process, for example, and then specific parts are assigned in an open "callback" which allows cast members (now guaranteed a place in the show) to play against one another.

The panel of judges at auditions also varies with the production, but it almost always includes the dramatic director, music director, choreographer, and producer, and it almost always calls for the auditioner to sing, act, and dance.

It is wise not to choose every crew member until the audition process is complete simply because an auditioner who fails to make the cast may be an excellent production assistant or backstage worker. This is especially true of school productions (secondary or college). Generally, however, crews are chosen from people skilled in the given area (lights, sound, make-up, etc.) by the directors responsible for that area. In a professional situation, crew members may come from a union list. In schools, they may be drawn from theatre tech classes or theatre clubs. Again, selection varies with the production environment.

The selection of orchestra members is also variable. It may be made from union lists, school performing groups, private contacts, or a combination of methods, and it is generally the province of the music director working under the financial constraints imposed by the producer.

Read-throughs. Once the staff, cast, crew, and pit have been chosen, it is time to bring them into contact with their material. That is the purpose of read-throughs. Here libretto and score are "performed" in a first viewing. Actors note their entrances and exits; technical cues are discussed; changes or modifications of the printed page are introduced. It is a time when each participant gets a feel for the forest before tackling any particular tree. Many read-throughs dispense with having the pit musicians play or the actors sing, preferring to introduce the music via solo piano or long-playing record. Some directors even prefer to read the libretto to the cast (as opposed to having each person play his or her own part) so that any desired directorial judgments or inflections can be made known from the outset. Just how read-throughs are handled depends upon the directors involved, and the variety possible is less important than that the read-throughs take place at all.

Rehearsals. Rehearsals go through several cycles during a well-organized production. At the beginning, tasks are separated and mastered individually. Scenes are blocked, dialogue coached, characterizations honed in drama rehearsals. Orchestras are trained at instrumental rehearsals. Singers work at vocal rehearsals. Sets are built and painted in a shop or on the stage. Dancers work on their material isolated from the rest of the production, using tapes or a piano for music. Lighting and sound crews set and test their equipment.

Once each facet has been mastered, the many pieces of the production jigsaw are brought together for technical integration. This forms the second rehearsal cycle, and it is often the most crucial. Finally, when all the interfacing edges of the production have been fitted together, run-throughs take place to work and rework continuity until the show is a well-oiled machine. During the interface and run-through stages of a production, the directors must cooperate with each other, and the cast must be patient and understanding. Failure on these accounts often spells disaster for a show. Those who cannot sublimate their egos to the well-being of the entire production or who do not complete initial work on time prevent integration and make run-throughs all but impossible.

Exactly how much time each phase of the rehearsal process should have depends upon the nature of the show. Generally, the initial phase and integration phase should have about the same amount of time. Run-throughs usually require less time. A ten-week school production, for example, might use four weeks for initial work, four weeks for integration, and two for run-throughs. Those proportions generally hold for most production environments.

Pre-performance production items. It is during the early phases of rehearsals that the producer usually attends to the more pressing business on his list of things to do. Generally, this includes ordering his tickets, arranging the procedures by which they will be sold, carrying out his publicity campaign, and printing his programs and playbills. These tasks often require others. Ticket-printing, for example, necessitates numbering aisles and seats, perhaps drawing up seating charts. In order to print programs, data on cast and staff must first be collected, advertising space sold, perhaps some artwork commissioned. Then, too, printers must be chosen, publicity distributed to media, advertising plans implemented. It is all quite a lot to do and very variable according to the production.

As opening night approaches, new production items become more pressing. Concession booths must be stocked and manned; ushers hired; security, fire, and parking needs accounted for; and, finally, the banking mechanism for handling and distributing income from ticket and concession sales must be established. All these require a timetable which is part of the calendar of any well-run show. To the extent they are not properly managed, the entire show suffers. For certain items—publicity, for example—poor management can kill a show outright.

The performance phase.　Once run-throughs are over, the show is ready to play as a full-fledged production. Many opening night performances are preceded by previews which not only help to work out last minute bugs, but also allow nervous casts and directors some space to tame an anxious soul. Previews often take place with specially invited audiences. They may even occur at an "out of town" theatre as a kind of trial run before the critics descend.

Eventually, however, the critics do descend, and the musical opens for real. From this point on, everything depends either on the contracts or the reviews. Performing rights contracts or limited-run agreements will dictate a finite number of performances. Reviews will determine, in most cases, whether the show will play on or fold. If a hit, the production may continue with plans for movie and/or TV rights, road shows, cast albums, and lots of financial wealth-distributing. If a flop, outstanding debts will be paid, theatres closed, personnel released, and wounds licked aplenty.

Ending procedures.　Hit or flop, all productions end (except, perhaps 'The Fantasticks'), and at such a point there are things to do: cast parties, set dismantling, equipment and material return, final accounting, to name just a few. Again, the items here depend upon the production itself and the environment in which it has occurred.

Suggested activity

Choose a musical and a production environment of your own and establish a production calendar with actual dates. Use the list of events below as a guide.

1. *Auditions*

    a.　Pre-audition publicity
    b.　Audition process (describe, give dates)

2. *Selection of crews* (enumerate each crew)

3. *Read-throughs*

4. *Rehearsals*

    a.　Initial learning phase (list what you wish done and when)
    b.　Integration phase (list what you wish done and when)

    c. Technical run-throughs
    d. Final run-throughs

5. *Pre-performance production items* (list the dates)

    a. Seating plans
    b. Ticket printing
    c. Program/playbill printing
    d. Publicity (describe what you wish done)
    e. Ticket sales (where and by whom)
    f. Concessions (food, parking, etc.)
    g. Ushers
    h. Security
    i. Miscellaneous (describe any other item you list)

6. *Previews*

7. *Performances*

8. *Accounting and banking (how done, by whom, when)*

9. *Ending procedures*

    a. Cast parties
    b. Set dismantling
    c. Return of equipment/materials
    d. Future plans (list, if any)

PART III

The Elements of Craftsmanship: Evaluating A Musical

INTRODUCTORY REMARKS

Thus far, we have looked at the historical development of the American musical and some of the more basic aspects of musical production. In this section we will consider the aesthetic properties of a show. What makes for a good show? How does one judge any given production. What are the things an author, director, or performer can do to insure an excellent product?

In dealing with these topics, it is paramount to understand the difference between the objective evaluation of craft and the subjective reaction one may have to the material at hand—in short, the difference between the statements "it is good" and "I like it."

Consider, for the moment, not a musical but a food—say, vanilla ice cream. A person can evaluate the ice cream both by how it is made and by how he or she reacts to it. If the ingredients are pure, of high quality, mixed and tended with care, packaged in a spotless plant with constant controls, the ice cream will in all likelihood be excellent ice cream, well-made ice cream. One might accurately say of it, "that is good ice cream." But suppose the person judging the ice cream doesn't like the flavor vanilla. No matter how well-made the product, that person must say "I don't like it." It is possible to appreciate the craftsmanship which produced the ice cream without enjoying the taste of the stuff. It is also possible to enjoy the taste of vanilla ice cream even if the manufacturer cut corners here and there in the production process. In such a case one might easily say, "that is not good, but I like it anyway."

So it is with a work of art—in our case, a musical production. One may like a poorly crafted work, not like a well-crafted work, or mix personal opinion and objective evaluation in many other ways. For the average theatre-goer, an understanding of these principles may be interesting but it is not critical to the viewing of a show. For the artists producing the theatrical product, however, it is indeed critical, just as it is critical for the cook who makes the vanilla ice cream to know precisely why ice cream is good or bad (that is, well-made or poorly made), whether or not he personally appreciates the flavor vanilla.

You are the cook—or at least one of the cooks—of a theatrical broth. It is imperative for you to know what makes that broth good or bad. You must know the proper ingredients to use, the right and wrong ways of blending them, the appropriate and inappropriate ways of seasoning them. You must know how to judge yourself and the production you create as a craftsman, not merely a reactive consumer.

Eventually, you will probably find, as many well-studied artists do, that your knowledge of craft and your subjective reactions begin to work in tandem. You will *like* something *because* it is well-crafted or *not* like it because it is *poorly* made. To the extent that both critics and audiences are aware of craft, they, too, become more perceptive and discriminating consumers. Hopefully, as each element of the theatrical community (author, director, actor, critic, audience) is educated to the understanding of theatrical craftsmanship, the standards of productions will rise. For now, it is your task to learn what the elements of good musical craftsmanship are, and the

54. *Introductory Remarks*

pages below, in a general way, will help introduce the topic.

A. EVALUATING DIRECTORIAL JUDGMENTS

We will begin our investigation of craft by looking at those decisions which were made by producer and director(s). What did they involve, and when they were made, were they conducive to excellence or counterproductive?

Choice of show. In critiquing a production or deciding whether or not you wish to be involved, you must first determine if the choice of material and the production environment are conducive to excellence. Does the show say something of value? Is it appropriate to the talent pool and location with which it interacts? Has it the financial resources capable of realizing its aims? Is the production staff competent?

I once saw a junior high school production of *'Oklahoma!,'* and I remember thinking as I drove to the school, "how in the world is a ninth-grader ever going to project the part of Jud? How can young kids pull off the ballet at the end of Act I? Given the scarcity of boys in junior high choruses, how will they ever cast the supporting roles and crowd sequences?" By the end of scene I, the answers to my questions were painfully clear. They could do nothing needed for a good production. The talent pool and environment were simply unable to support the material. It was an embarrassing evening for performers and audience alike. The directorial judgment—or should I say misjudgment—in choosing *'Oklahoma!'* had doomed the production from its inception. So many other shows might have fared better in this environment: *'You're a Good Man, Charlie Brown,' 'L'il Abner,' 'Bye, Bye, Birdie!,'* to name just three. Why had the directors not seen that *'Oklahoma!,'* certainly a fine musical property, could never reveal any of its greatness in that particular setting?

As you involve yourself in your own productions, think carefully about the material itself. Try not to rush into a show just because it has a glamourous title or a particular person associated with it. Be as discriminating with your musical associations as you ought to be with your personal ones. There is an Italian adage which, roughly translated, says, "show me who you walk with, and I'll tell you what you are." It is a very wise saying for judging the selection of a show.

Choice of theatre. *'The Fantasticks'* is an intimate show, and to play well it needs an intimate theatre. Put it in a hall seating fifteen hundred, and it would more than likely be swallowed up. On the other hand, shows like *'Camelot'* require a measure of grandeur. They need large stages, ample sets, and glittering costumes to achieve the effects for which they are intended.

The second element of directorial judgment to consider is how well the production has been wedded to its physical environment. This is a decision which is not only aesthetic. It has direct financial overtones as well. Small theatres mean fewer possible ticket sales. Larger ones mean more. Directors and producers who choose the right hall for their musicals must then decide how much per ticket they will charge, how many performances they will have, and what kind of production budget they can sustain.

Use of the stage. Once the hall has been chosen, the next thing to look for in judging a show is the use of the stage itself. Have the sets been placed so that every seat has a view of every scene? Is the staging compatible with the physical structure of the theatre? Is it compatible with the aesthetic ambiance of the show? Is the full playing area being employed?

We have already seen how the inventive staging of the revival of *'Candide'* sparked a successful Broadway run. There are many other such examples. The Northstage dinner theatre in Glen Cove, Long Island had an interesting assignment in its production of *'Oliver.'* The theatre was a large proscenium hall with good viewing angles but rather limited wing and fly space. With such a configuration, it was difficult to change scenes rapidly, and *'Oliver'* calls for several locations, some of which (like the funeral parlor) appear only once during the production. The staging problems were solved by building a huge turntable on which various locations were set. By rotating the turntable—in full sight of the audience—scenes were changed in a matter of seconds. Characters walked and talked as the stage carousel swung around so that one scene blended into another with nary a blackout or pause. The technique was not only perfect for the hall but ideally suited to the episodic nature of the writing as well. Like turning the pages of the original novel, this *'Oliver'* transported its audience from scene to scene with both intelligence and creativity.

The turntable is but one of many ways to mount a set which integrates with hall and show. Building a thrust beyond the proscenium, raking a stage to slant upward as it goes back from the audience, building extensions or ramps from stage to audience, playing in the round, using an open set with characters changing scenery and area lighting to highlight locations are all methods which can be employed. The question is, should they be employed, and if they are, do they help the production? Do they improve the flow of action, deepen the involvement of the audience, enable the viewer to see the action more clearly, use all the available playing area wisely?

Blocking. Closely allied to the use of the stage is the way in which action is blocked. Blocking refers to the positioning of actors as any given scene unfolds. Where people are placed and how they move from place to place is extremely important because it helps to define the production both visually and dramatically. Let us investigate this last statement more closely since it contains concepts fundamental to all theatre.

The theatre is an art form which exists in both time and space. It molds time through the development of plot and character. It organizes space through the placement of animate and inanimate objects. Because it has these properties inherent to its nature, it communicates not only aurally through sound but visually as well. To a very large extent, it asks its audience to react aesthetically to a series of images which flow one to another.

Just as a painter must deal with the balance and form of a canvas in creating a stationary picture, a director must deal with balance and form in positioning actors, props, and sets. The visualization of the action—even divorced from the meaning of the action—has a profound aesthetic effect upon the viewer. But even more, it has an important relationship to the dramatic content as well because the placement and movement of actors relative to each other and to the set helps them to define their characters and tell their story.

If one character, for example, wishes to dominate another (think of the relationship between the King and Anna in *'The King and I'*), he can be blocked so that visually he is taller, or more prominent, or closer to the audience. The pictures thus formed may not only be pretty (that is, have shapes on the stage which are aesthetically striking), but they may also help to convey a dramatic meaning, in this case, a relationship between characters.

In evaluating the blocking of a show, then, you should ask two questions: did it enhance the aesthetic, visual effect of the production, and did it help to convey the dramatic content of the work?

Pacing and architecture.   Nothing can so quickly distinguish an amateurish director from a professional one as his handling of pacing and dramatic architecture. Pacing refers to the flow of the action not only within a scene but from one scene to another. Dramatic architecture refers to the way in which emotions are sculpted within scenes and cumulatively across the breadth of an entire act or an entire production. They are elements which are allied not only to each other but to things like set design, staging, and blocking as well. We will discuss each in turn.

Consider the rumor scene from *'Fiddler on the Roof.'* In song and action, one character rushes up to the next excitedly relaying incorrect information about various members of the village of Anatevka. The words tumble over one another. "Do you know about Perchik, the student from Kiev?..." "Remember the wedding?..." "Well, I just heard that Golde's been arrested!..." On and on they go until the entire effect reaches a kind of comic climax. To pace this scene leisurely would ruin it. Its tempo should be like lightning in order to fit its character. If it is paced slowly, it will drag and lose its audience.

On the other hand, consider the moment when in *'West Side Story'* Tony and Maria meet in the midst of a crowded, boisterous dance held in the gym of a slum settlement house. Their environment fades away and slowly they see the room with the fantasy of newly introduced lovers. They walk toward each other and dance. To pace this moment with speed would be to make it grotesquely comical. If anything, the director's job here is to reduce the flow of performance adrenalin so that the audience can linger over the magic which occurs when two people fall in love. It is, after all, this moment upon which the relationship between Tony and Maria and all of the subsequent action of the musical are built. Rushing it would be criminal.

Nor does pacing refer only to the events within a scene. It also reveals itself in the tempo with which one scene follows another. I once attended a high school production of *'South Pacific,'* a show which calls for several locations. The production was mounted on a proscenium stage which had limited fly and wing space. The set design called for rather large flats and bulky, heavy furniture. The result of this mixture of theatrical ingredients was a tedious, amateurish cocktail. Nellie and Emile finish a tender romantic moment after which a blackout occurs. Then, in veiled stage shadows, we see the figures of frantic crew members clunking off the plantation set and rushing to put on the army compound of a war-torn island. Bang. Crash. Titters from the audience. The mood is broken; the wait for the next piece of action, interminable. Compare this to the turntable set of *'Oliver'* described earlier. What a difference in pacing.

As a rule of thumb, anything longer than ten seconds between scenes is too long—especially for modern audiences weaned on the instant location changes of television and motion pictures. It is the job of the production staff (particularly set designer and drama director) to come up with a plan which paces the musical professionally.

Now draw a rectangle. Let its height represent the emotional pitch of a given scene, its length, the time it takes for the scene to unfold. Within this framework, chart the architecture of what you are studying or performing. If the line graph you draw is flat, you may be assured your audience will be bored. If your graph is undulated with clearly defined goals of motion, you may be sure your audience is absorbed in the action (see below).

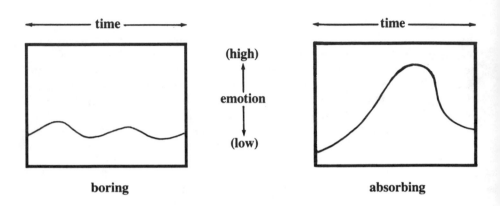

boring   **absorbing**

Theatre, like life itself, is a medium which exists in time. If nothing happens to mark the flow of time—to shape it and give it measurement—it loses its meaning. Many things can provide that shape: events, developments of character, changes of location. Without some motion, however, the passage of theatrical time is purposeless.

It is the job of the writer and director to sculpt theatrical time so that it has motion and interest. We will see later in our discussion of the elements of good writing how things like conflict and character development can do this. Since our focus right now is on the judgments of the director, we can observe that pacing, blocking, and architectural awareness all help shape the events within a scene and the total accumulation of scenes within a musical. Not only is this true of the action in terms of dialogue and blocking but of the musical numbers as well, and later we will discuss in detail the tension-release mechanisms which lie behind well-sculpted music.

The graphic examples above are, of course, not the only shapes possible. Good scenes can start on a high pitch and work downward just as well as they can build to a crescendo from a quiet beginning. They can have several goals of motion, and many variations are possible. What they cannot have, however, is a posture of extremes. If there is no motion at all, it will not matter if the pitch is high or low. Without contrast, discernible shape is impossible. If, on the other hand, there is an incessant wobbling from calm to climax to calm to climax, the effect of any one moment of calm or any one moment of climax will be reduced to nothingness because there will be nothing special about it.

Casting and the use of personnel. The last important area in the evaluation of directorial judgment is that of casting and the utilization of on-stage and off-stage personnel. In some respects it is easy to evaluate these things; in others, it is extremely difficult.

The physical manifestations of casting are readily apparent. One does not put a midget in the role of a romantic lead, for example, or pair a six-foot-six-inch Jack with a four-foot-eleven Jill. More subtle, however, are questions of "typing." Have the natural propensities (physical and non-physical) of the actors been well-married to the roles chosen for them? Have the demands of characterization made upon the actors coincided with their abilities? These are things less able to be judged by a casual onlooker. They are best evaluated by those who know the cast personally and professionally.

Still more complex are the sociological manifestations of casting. Consider the revival of *'The Pajama Game'* which occurred well after the civil rights movement of the 1960's. When it pit Hal Linden, a white romantic male lead, opposite Barbara McNair, a black romantic female lead, it may have raised a conservative eyebrow, but on the Broadway stage of that time it was not a social shock severe enough to impede the flow of the musical. What, however, might the repercussions of such casting have been if the setting were Savannah, Georgia in the 1920's?

Finally, hidden entirely from casual view but nonetheless crucial to the theatrical product is the rapport established between the director and those he directs. Was the relationship tyrannical or an artistic partnership? Did the managerial style behind the scenes get the most from the cast and crew or did it leave large measures of talent unutilized? In considering this area, it is best not to leap to conclusions or to be prejudiced by methods of working which appeal personally to you.

The complex mix of personalities in a musical production is rarely satisfied by one directorial approach. Some people need a kick in the pants to give their best; others may require a bit of babying; still others may respond best by being left alone. Differentiated styles of management are usually the most successful because they can adapt to the variety of personalities and situations which inevitably arise in a musical production.

Skilled directors must not only know their art, they must know how to read and handle people. They must be part parent, part friend, part taskmaster, part psychiatrist, part teacher, part dictator. Above all, they must be able to exercise their judgments for the well-being of the entire production. They can't be so tyrannical that they alienate their workforce nor so wishy-washy that they leave critical decisions unattended. Finally, they and every other member of the production family must ultimately bend thoughts of self to thoughts of show. "I" must become "we" in the mind of each participant to have a truly excellent effort. Egocentricity and selfishness have no place in good theatre.

Suggested activities

1.   Attend a musical being produced somewhere nearby and evaluate the directorial judgments behind the production.

   a.   Was the choice of show a good one for the environment?
   b.   Were the show and theatre well-suited to each other?
   c.   How was the stage used? Would you have done anything differently? What and why?

     d.   Criticize the blocking. What was effective about it? What was ineffective?

     e.   How was the show paced? If pacing and architecture were poor, what would you have done to improve them?

     f.   Was the show well-cast? Discuss the major characters. Did the actors make them convincing?

    2.   Now choose a scene from a musical and put it on yourself (minus costumes, props, etc.).

     a.   Did you choose a scene appropriate to your environment and theatre?

     b.   Did you cast it as well as you could given your talent pool?

     c.   Did the blocking and architecture make for an absorbing performance?

    3.   The opening scene of 'South Pacific' calls for many moods and some interesting characterizations. How might you adapt it to your theatre and talent pool? If it is not easily adaptable to your situation, choose two hypothetical environments and compare how you would do it in each. Set it in the round for a professional summer stock production, for instance. Now put it on the proscenium stage of a high school. What changes will you have to make to have a well-cast, well-paced scene in both instances?

B. EVALUATING MUSICAL PERFORMANCE

The important musical elements in judging a show are the quality of solo singing; the quality of ensemble singing; the quality of instrumental playing; the blend between voices and instruments; and the way in which things like tempi, dynamics, and musical architecture have been handled.

The quality of solo singing. There seems to be a school of thought that somehow the elements of good singing (proper posture, diaphragmatic breathing, accuracy of pitch, accuracy of intonation, rhythmic precision, good diction, projection, good tonal quality, proper use of vibrato, etc.) are reserved for opera, oratorio, or art song and are not necessary in the musical theatre. That, of course, is nonsense. They are fundamental to good singing anywhere. What is true is that in the musical theatre one must also know how to sing as a character and how to pace one's voice across the demands of a performance night after night.

Many times performers are asked to sacrifice good vocal production by the directors of a musical to achieve a style of singing which has become known in the trade as the "Broadway belt." I believe this to be not only artistically unnecessary but physically cruel as well. Any musical director or performer who thinks that the raucous squawk of the Broadway belt is conducive either to good theatre or to the longevity of one's career ought to have his head examined.

With that said, good solo singing in a musical requires putting good vocal production to work in the service of one's character, and that will mean different things depending upon the character. Consider *'Oklahoma!,'* for example, and the difference between Laurie and Ado Annie. Laurie is a romantic lead, Ado Annie, a comic supporting character. The heavy twang of the Oklahoma Territory can easily be overdone in Laurie's solo numbers, making songs like "People Will Say We're in Love" and "Many a New Day" caricatures as opposed to love songs. The twang, however, is just perfect for Ado Annie's "I'm Just a Girl Who Can't Say No" and "All or Nothing." It intensifies her role as a comedienne, sets her in sharper contrast to Laurie, and keeps her characterization consistent from speech to song.

Consider the demands upon Liza Doolittle in *'My Fair Lady.'* As a guttersnipe she must perform in dialect. "Just you wite, 'enry 'iggins," she sings, her cockney dripping from every phrase. But as the Dutchess of the Embassy Ball she must sing "I could have danced all night" with the diction and dialect of royalty. In fact, the entire purpose of her character, indeed, of the musical itself, depends upon her juxtaposing Liza, the street girl, with Eliza, the lady.

Lastly, consider the character of Professor Higgins in the same show. His glib, self-assured cockiness is captured in patter songs which hardly require him to sing at all. His material is more spoken recitation demanding rhythmic precision and the ability to go in and out of song by touching a note here and there. To try to sing as Curley sings in *'Oklahoma!'* would destroy the character of Higgins and work at cross-purposes to his music.

The quality of ensemble singing.   The vocal techniques of good ensemble sing-ing are essentially the same as those for the solo voice. To these techniques one must also consider the blending of parts and cohesion of rhythm and diction when judging the choral aspects of a musical. Be aware as you evaluate ensemble singing that much depends upon the choral writing itself. Production numbers which include a full cast may range from simple unison singing (like that in "Consider Yourself" from *'Oliver'*) to complex multipart singing (like that found in the title song of *'Oklahoma!'*). Final-ly, it is neither unheard of nor unwise for musical directors to rearrange the choral writing of a musical to better fit the production environment. The divisi scoring of the original version of *'Oklahoma!,'* for example, is beyond most high school stage choirs. Simplifying it can render it singable without harming the musical integrity of the show. Your evaluations should take such matters into consideration.

The quality of instrumental playing.   Evaluations of instrumental playing are rather straightforward. Did the instruments play in tune? Were they rhythmically precise? Did they hit the right notes? Again, be careful to assess the difficulty of the orchestrations themselves in making these judgments. The scores to *'Candide,'* *'West Side Story,'* and *'Man of La Mancha,'* for example, are notoriously more difficult than the average musical. Pits which tackle them should therefore be judged accord-ingly. Finally, just as it may be wise to rearrange difficult choral writing for some production environments, it may be wise to do the same for the orchestra. In fact, it may be downright imperative. Few school orchestras, for example, can boast a full complement of competent players. Indeed, the size of the pit itself may dictate cutting down the number of orchestral parts for physical if not musical reasons. In recent years the performing rights agencies which rent out orchestra parts along with the scripts and vocal books of a show have even taken to offering their clients a choice of orchestrations. If you are doing *'The Sound of Music,'* for example, you may re-quest any of three versions: the original full orchestration, a reduced orchestration, or a two-piano accompaniment. A knowledge of all these factors should govern the decisions of the production staff and your evaluations of them and of the performances they engender.

The blend between voices and instruments.   The lower range of both alto and bass voices tends to project with far less gusto than their upper ranges. Tenors, especial-ly school tenors, frequently have problems with the notes above their high F. Sopranos may from time to time have difficulty an octave or so above middle C, the spot where many of them break from chest to head tone resonance. Orchestral scoring which is insensitive to these and other vocal problems will ultimately render the voices in-audible. And there are more things which can disturb the balance between instruments and voices: a poor sound system, inadequate miking, a hall with poor acoustics, an insensitive conductor—to name just a few.

In judging the blend and balance between instruments and voices, one rule must remain cardinal: the clarity and understandability of the voice takes precedence over all other concerns. It is only in the overture or dance music that the pit can function without concern for the spoken or sung word. In the songs and underdialogue scor-ing of a musical, nothing should be done to render the voice inaudible. Directors who do not understand or accede to this principle work at cross-purposes to the medium of live theatre, and can only be considered wrong in their judgments.

The best directors are the ones who understand this principle and who can reshape orchestrations, sound systems, staging, or the music itself (through wiser choices of key or better vocal arrangements) to effect the communication necessary for a good musical performance.

Aesthetic musical judgments.   Finally, in evaluating the musical performance of a production, one must take into account the aesthetic decisions of the music director(s). Were the tempi too slow, too fast, or just right? Were the dynamics balanced between loud and soft so that the musical had contrast and interest or were things too monochromatic and dull? Did the musical numbers have architectural shape or were they lifeless and repetitive?

Remember as you make these evaluations that only so much can be done by the performers and directors. A good deal is the function of the composer, lyricist, and librettist, and later in this chapter we will investigate some of the properties of good writing which aid the performers long before the opening night curtain. In fact, it is wise always to remember that a good musical really requires a confluence of four streams: good writing, good directing, good performing, and good production.

Suggested activities

1.   Listen to the original cast album of *'My Fair Lady.'* How do Julie Andrews as Liza, Rex Harrison as Higgins, and Stanley Holloway as Alfred P. Doolittle reveal their characters in their singing?

2.   Listen to the original cast albums of both *'Brigadoon'* and *'Candide.'* Discuss the quality of the choral singing you hear, particularly in numbers like ''Brigadoon'' and ''Make Our Garden Grow.''

3.   Compare the ensemble singing you have heard in item #2 above with the singing of ''Matchmaker'' from the original cast album of *'Fiddler on the Roof.'* Discuss your observations and evaluations.

4.   Compare the singing of Ezio Pinza in the original *'South Pacific'* cast album to that of Robert Preston in the album of *'The Music Man.'* How does each performer reveal his character in song? Do you think each is successful?

5.   Now choose a character and a song for yourself from an established musical. Discuss how you plan to perform the song. What tempo is right? Will you sing in dialect? What will you do with dynamics to help sculpt the architecture of the song? Would you need miking if you were singing against the original orchestration? Given the limits of your environment, perform your song for others and discuss their reactions to you.

6.   Finally, given the character of your environment, choose an ensemble number for performance. Discuss not only how you plan to sing it but also how you might stage it. Perform it for an audience of some kind and discuss the reactions you get.

C. EVALUATING DRAMATIC PERFORMANCE

The evaluation of dramatic performance depends on one's understanding of the elements which go into characterization and its realization in any given moment on the stage. To some extent, we have already touched upon this topic in our discussion of solo singing. It is now time for us to probe it in a bit more depth.

Characterization in general. Michael Chekhov, the great director, writes in his book *To the Actor* (New York: Harper and Row, 1953) that good acting is the ability to manifest the inner psychology of a character in overt physical terms. Truer words were never spoken. The trick is to know how to do it, and in the pages below we will investigate some things which may be of use.

1. *Psychological analysis.* People live not so much in their surface actions but in the unseen world of their inner thoughts and feelings. They love; they hope; they fear; they dream. They are stimulated or bored. They are aware or unaware. In fact, it is this unseen world which determines their surface actions. A man sits in an easy chair, reading. We watch him. He stirs, puts his book down, rises, and walks to a water pitcher. He fills it and drinks, then resumes his position to continue reading. We see only the surface motion of his being. The feelings of thirst which drove his every action are hidden from view.

In shaping a character, the actor must try to understand—or invent—the inner psychology of that character. Fagin may walk with a stoop in *'Oliver.'* Why does he stoop? Could it simply be because he was born that way? Yes, it could. And if that is what the actor playing him believes, the next question is "how does Fagin feel about his walk?" Is he indifferent? But perhaps the condition was not there by birth. Perhaps it is an occupational deformity caused by years of hunching over the counting table, hoarding stolen coins in his thieves' lair. If so, the deformity is more a product of his psychology than the cause of it. How then does he feel about it? Or perhaps he doesn't stoop at all. If not, why not?

There is little any of us do which is not shaped by the inner person. The jobs we hold, what we eat, the relationships we form, the way we walk and talk—they are all the surface manifestations of an unseen world. To build a convincing character, to be a convincing actor, one must first tap that world.

2. *An awareness of dimensionality.* In investigating the psychology of a given character it is wise to remember that rarely, if ever, are people wholly one thing or wholly another. We all have our good points and our weaknesses, and any true assessment of us takes all positives and negatives into account before rendering a final balance. So it should also be with the characterizations we create. Rarely, if ever, is a given character the embodiment of pure evil or pure good, pure innocence or pure guile.

Consider some of the more intriguing characters of the musical theatre. Professor

Higgins in *'My Fair Lady'* is rough and ill-tempered, but he dares to speak the truth in a hypocritical world, and he is genuinely devoted to Eliza's development. Tevye in *'Fiddler on the Roof'* is obstinate and domineering, but never did a man so love his family or lavish such reverence and devotion to his God, albeit with a sassy tongue and impudent wit. Madame Rose in *'Gypsy'* is as neurotic a stage mother as ever trod the earth, but when Herbie walks out on her, her heart is truly broken and we can see that she loves him even though she cannot consummate her love with a stable, permanent relationship. The kind and gentle Anna in *'The King and I'* is nonetheless capable of anger and obstinacy in her relationship with the King.

True, these characters are dimensional in large measure because they were created by writers who gave them that dimension. Actors are always to some extent—perhaps a large extent—dependent upon authors for the strength of their material. But they must also be able to realize the potential of the material, even rise above it when it is inferior. Doing that requires a dimensional vision of a character. Thus, the assessment of the psychological underpinning of a character should be dimensional as well.

3. *Exceptions to dimensionality.* While the dimensional character is desirable in most cases, there are times when stereotypes or archetypes are called for, and that is because there are kinds of theatre which are not representational.

Most theatre mirrors reality in more or less real terms. People are on the stage what they are in real life; they do in the context of the play more or less what they do in the everyday world. Such theatre is called representational theatre, and in representational theatre dimensional characterization is appropriate because it better reflects the real world. By the way, that is even true of representational theatre which uses techniques like timelessness or the presentation of thought in action. Willy Loman in Arthur Miller's *Death of a Salesman,* for example, is a dimensional character in an essentially representational play even though we travel through the visualization of his thoughts from reality to fantasy, from past to present. People, after all, do fantasize, and the overt visualization of such fantasy is still part of representational drama. To use a parallel example, what we see of Willy in *Death of a Salesman* we also see of Don Quixote in *'Man of La Mancha.'* The treatment of the whore Dulcinea as a noble lady or the windmills of La Mancha as giant demons are illustrations of the Don's fantasies. Their depiction in representational theatre is not itself a fantasy.

However, in story theatre or allegorical theatre or what we have come to call the "theatre of the absurd" in twentieth century writing, the aim is not to represent reality, and so dimensional characterization is not called for. In fact, it may work at cross-purposes to the theatrical style. In plays like Samuel Beckett's *Waiting for Godot* or Edward Albee's *The American Dream,* characters are enlargements of reality rather than mirrors of it. They are exaggerations which would lose their point if placed within the less stereotypical mold of real individuals.

The use of the archetype character is not confined to the stage. Consider a novel like Herman Melville's *Billy Budd* where Billy is the epitome of good and Claggart the epitome of evil. Indeed, it is one of Melville's many points in the novel to show us that neither Billy nor Claggart can survive for long in the real world, and it is an interesting literary technique for him to do so by pitting both archetypes against the context of dimensional men in a realistic setting.

To return to the musical, now consider the characters in *'Candide'* and *'The Fantasticks.'* Candide and Cunegonde, Matt and Louisa, Dr. Pangloss and El Gallo are not meant to be real people. They are every young couple in love, or the voice of Fate, or the instrument of Providence, and they appear and appeal to us as stereotypes precisely because they are part of a non-representational world. They are what they are through the magic of theatrical fantasy. To make them dimensional would be to rob them of the essence of that fantasy, to turn the fantasy into a mirror of reality.

When playing such a role or evaluating such a character, it is very important to distinguish between the demands of representational theatre and those of non-representational theatre. The first deals in dimensional characterization; the second, by definition, does not.

4. *Growth and change in characterization.* It is a rare individual who remains unmoved by the passage of time, unchanged by the peaks and valleys of human existence. Life demands change, and, in the course of living it, we all grow from what we were at birth to what we are at death. So, too, with the characters we depict. It is a poor play (and we shall discuss "why" later on in this chapter) which leaves its characters the same at the end of the script as they were in the beginning. For the actor and director it is important to be aware that change is necessary and to reveal that change in the process of portrayal. Let us consider, by way of example, some of the characters we touched upon earlier.

Tevye, the milkman in *'Fiddler...,'* is hardly the same person at the end of Act II that he was at the opening curtain. Once self-assured and confident in the order of the world and his place in it, he is now shaken. His home is gone; his traditions are all but gone; his family is scattered. He is anything but confident, anything but self-assured. Now he clings to his faith not simply for a reassurance of order but for survival itself. That is quite a metamorphosis. And Higgins in *'My Fair Lady?'* From an independent man content to remain alone, he changes into a person who knows he is incomplete without Eliza's love. Eliza's change is, of course, overtly dramatic, from guttersnipe to beauty, from self-effacing street urchin to self-confident lady. In *'The King and I,'* the King dies and Anna has changed in her attitude from defiance to an understanding which borders on love. In *'The Music Man,'* Hill changes from con man to Honest John.

Over and over we see the principle operating, and in assessing and depicting a characterization, along with all the other factors, one must account for change.

Surface manifestations of characterization. The intellectual awareness of building one's character is, of course, only half the battle. The other half is creating the overt physical reality, and here there is much to absorb the actor and much to judge in others. The inner being of a character is revealed in several ways: walk and general movement, speech, physiological idiosyncracies apart from walk and speech, use of props. Before looking at these specifics, however, it is necessary to say a word about how each aspect of physical characterization is affected by the three dimensions of physical performance: weight, space, and time.

1. *Weight, space, and time.* By weight we mean the degree to which the law of gravity seems to affect a given character. By space we refer to the physical territory the character commands in his or her actions. By time we mean the pace with which those actions occur. Each of these dimensions is applied to the movement and speech of a character in such a way as to reveal the inner psychology of the character.

To the extent the actor and director are skilled, the application of weight, space, and time will reveal much and be of great use. In less skilled hands they may be only intermittently applied and reveal very little. Let us see how they work in specific situations using some of the characters mentioned above.

A person who is sure of himself entitles himself to a definite—usually broad— field of movement and speech. Tevye, at the outset of *'Fiddler,'* is such a person. His weight is heavy, solid. He feels the ground beneath his feet as surely as he feels the strength of his traditions. His space is large. He gestures outward, entitling himself to command more than simply the area of his body. Like a tough basketball center who claims ownership of the territory beneath the basket, Tevye's space extends away from the volume occupied by his frame. His tempo is deliberate. He is self-assured and feels no need to stammer or rush. His psychology is firm and so it follows that his speech will be firm. For Tevye, solid weight, broad space, and steady time are the keys to establishing a self-assured character.

But as Tevye's world is rent from him, as his traditions are broken, his family split apart, his village destroyed, he becomes less cocky and his weight, space, and time will change. As he tries to deceive his wife and himself, his steps will become lighter, his gestures less broad, his voice higher and more rapid, perhaps with a stammer or stutter. The changes of the world bring changes to his psychological being which in turn are reflected in changes of a physical nature.

Consider Higgins at the outset of *'My Fair Lady.'* Glib, cocky, thoroughly in control, and thoroughly imbued with himself. His demeanor is consummately solid. He neither rushes nor stammers in his tempo. His weight is sure; his space, definite, but perhaps, because of genteel breeding, not quite as broad as Tevye. When Eliza wounds him by leaving, however, his physical characteristics change. He slows to a crawl, pausing over things (like Eliza's chocolate or her records) which once he took for granted. His weight becomes ponderous for the world, which once seemed light enough for him to support, now hangs heavily on his shoulders. His space is less commanding because he is less commanding.

Without belaboring the point with further examples, it is nonetheless important to see weight, space, and time as three continua, not as three ingredients with only two extremes. Weight is not either heavy or light, but anything in between. Space is not narrow or broad, but a whole gamut of dimensions. Time is not fast or slow, but a range of pacings. Finally, characterizations are not built of one or two "settings" of the physical scales, but many settings which modulate through the action, depending upon what is happening and what effect the happenings have upon the character.

It is also important to note that moods and meanings will not require the same "settings" of weight, space, and time in different characters. Both Tevye and Higgins, for example, are self-assured men whose metamorphoses make them much less sure of themselves. Yet each man is different from the other in circumstance and location; therefore, "self-assuredness" will be revealed by different uses of weight, space and time for each.

Tevye is poor, essentially untutored, living in a rough environment. Higgins is cultured, educated, living in a pampered environment. The weight of Tevye is thus likely to be heavier than that of Higgins; his voice louder, less considerate; his manner more boisterous and thus the space he commands more broad. For him to show change, his voice may stutter and rise in pitch. For Higgins it may do just the opposite.

Glib speed and tenor certainty may turn to deliberate pace and a baritone weight which show that the world has defeated him.

All of these judgments are, of course, the province of actor and director. As you apply them to your work or evaluate them in others, you must decide what is appropriate to the character and the situation.

2. *Walk and movement.* People reveal themselves in the language of their bodies. The way they walk, sit, stand, and move demonstrates a view of themselves and of their world. The old man shuffles his legs because they are brittle and arthritic. The nervous young schoolmarm flits from position to position lest the permanent occupancy of space cause her to take a psychological stance as well as a physical one. The fat lady sits astride her chair unmindful of a womanly demeanor. The femme fatale is aware of every erotic fiber. She crosses her legs seductively and makes sure to undulate her hips as she walks.

The applications of weight, space, and time to the movement of a character are endless. Doing them well, with a sense of appropriateness, knowing what to use and when, where to overplay and where to underplay, are all matters of delicate judgment for actor and director. Sometimes they may happen after much thought and discussion. Sometimes they may arise out of spontaneous insight or even accident. In any case, they are there ready to help build a character or set a mood.

3. *Speech.* There are five principal ingredients to be used in shaping character through voice. They are: vocal quality, vocal pitch, tempo of speech, use of dialect, and the inflection given to any line.

Vocal quality refers to the overall character of the voice. Is it rough or smooth, for instance? Does it crackle with the rasp of an old person, or is it flowing and mellifluous? Does it have the airy flavor of a whisper, or is it fully resonant? Vocal pitch refers to how high or low the speech pattern is; tempo, as we have already seen, refers to how quickly or slowly the pace of the words occurs. Dialect is used to fix geographic regionalisms. Tevye will have a Russian flavor to his words; Fagin, a British accent denoting lower class speech. Finally, inflection will be used to fix the precise meaning or interpretation of a given line. Are the words "I love you," for example, to be inflected "I *love* you," or "I love *you*," or some other variant which more accurately reflects the situation at hand? Are they to be spoken with tenderness, disdain, indifference? The possibilities are almost inexhaustible.

Again, how the vocal techniques which are available are actually applied is up to actor and director. They are tools to be used or not used at any given moment.

4. *Other physical idiosyncracies.* Besides movement and speech, an actor can use other physical idiosyncracies to portray a role. Nervous tics, twitches, recurrent glances, etc., are frequently employed by knowledgeable craftsmen in the service of a characterization. I remember seeing a particularly good Fagin, for example, who adopted a certain wringing of the hands to convey an underlying nature of greed and usury. I knew a Captain Von Trapp who gave a cold, authoritarian air to his character by clasping his wrists behind him in a quasi-military manner. The possibilities for such things are as limitless as the imagination of the actor. They have only to be tried and applied appropriately to help build a memorable characterization. As to what "appropriately" means, again, that is a circumstantial matter which only the given situation

can fully define.

There are no rules for automatic application, no substitutes for the intelligent assessment of actor and director.

5. *Use of props.* Finally, physical characterization can be aided by the use of props. The classic example is Captain Queeg's toying with his steel ball bearings in *The Caine Mutiny,* but any prop can do. Eye glasses, a purse, a walking stick, a hat, a handkerchief, even a part of one's costume can be called into service. Often, an external prop can be the key which releases an entire characterization. I knew a little Gretl once in *'The Sound of Music'* who was just hideously ill at ease because she didn't know what to do on stage when she wasn't talking. After awhile, I decided to give her a little teddy bear to carry around. It was entirely appropriate to her character, and she took to it like a duck to water. It gave her something to do with her hands, something to look at, something to relate to when she was not directly involved in the action. Within a few weeks she had worked out several routines with the toy, all of which put her at ease, helped define her character, and enhanced the production.

What props you use or how you evaluate the use of props by others is, again, a matter for momentary judgment. Like all of the elements of physical characterization, it is a tool to be used or not used as one sees fit.

Characterization in action. Thus far we have discussed the elements of characterization in general, divorced from their application to the process of performance. When they are actually integrated into the flow of production, there are certain things the actor or critic must bear in mind.

The first of these is something called dramatic focus. At any given moment, there is one thing on the stage which is designed to capture the attention of the audience. That thing is known as the dramatic focus. Most often the focus is on the person or persons who are speaking, but it need hardly be limited to this alone. A sudden movement, a certain lighting effect, a pose staged in such a way as to be visually prominent, these are all capable of being the dramatic focus of a scene. Actually, the essence of the dramatic focal point is that it is different from its surrounding environment. Its difference causes it to stand out and thus to become noticed. In a crowd of moving actors, for example, the one person who freezes in a stationary pose becomes the dramatic focus. In a tableau of frozen positions, it is the person who moves that commands the focus.

In building a character successfully, it is most important to integrate that character with the changing focus of drama in any given scene. When the character is part of the dramatic focus, the elements of characterization become more prominent—not so much because the actor makes them so but because the audience perceives them as such. When the focus shifts from a character, his characterization is less prominent, and he must be careful to keep it up (although not so that it intrudes upon what is then the focus).

There is a tendency among poorer performers to stop acting, as it were, when the dramatic focus shifts from them. That is very disconcerting to the overall effect of a scene because it constantly destroys the illusion of the entire environment. The best actors are always in character no matter where the focus of attention lies. They actually listen to and watch the speaker; they actually relate to the actors near them.

This takes a tremendous amount of concentration. It forces a constant aesthetic commitment and requires a constant stream of energy, but it also yields enormous dividends by breathing life into an entire scene.

If an analogy would help in this area, consider the world of sports. In a football or baseball or basketball game (particularly the latter because movement is so continuous), the focus of attention is generally the ball. Whoever has it inherits the attention for as long as he possesses it. But the team members who are away from the ball are nonetheless still in the game, and if they fail to keep alert, to keep playing, they will realize very little of their potential. Either they will not be ready when the ball comes to them or they will not anticipate plays whose success depends upon their moving without the ball. In basketball particularly (and also in soccer and hockey), movement away from the ball (or puck) is one of the hallmarks of a professional. In acting, maintaining the integrity of one's character when not in dramatic focus is a similar sign of professionalism.

In a musical, the maintenance of character is required not only in drama but also in song. We have already discussed how important it is to be able to preserve one's character in solo singing. It is equally important in ensemble singing when the focus of attention may be directed elsewhere or diffused across the panoply of large scale production stagings. In song as well as drama, the principle is the same, and it is vital to the overall effect of the action.

The second ingredient the actor or critic must bear in mind in integrating character with production is the element of timing. It is one thing to say your lines in the isolation of a dressing room. It is another to say them in the context of a real performance. The first, while it may be perfect in vocal and physical characterization, nonetheless lacks the element of integration with other people or with the set and props. This integration requires a constant timing between events. Should the lines tumble over one another? Should the actor "take a beat" to pause for inflection or meaning?

It is said that timing is everything and that it really cannot be taught. In part that is true. Timing is certainly crucial to the pacing and architecture of a scene, and there is no doubt that some gifted actors are born with a genius for knowing just how long to wait or how much to rush. Like phrasing in a musical performance, however, timing can be coached, and over the years, with much observation and theatrical analysis, one's timing can be sharpened. Again, there are no rules for good timing because dramatic situations are so variable. The judgments which you make in this area as a performer or the criticisms you have of the timing of others will simply have to stand or fall on the merits of the moment.

One thing which aids the timing of the actor is, of course, familiarity with the script. Knowing what one is going to say and where one is going to move is indispensable to the pace of saying it or getting there. It is therefore wise to know not just your lines, but everyone's lines, not just your blocking, but everyone's blocking. It is also wise to know the meaning of the lines or scene, not just the lines themselves. If you know, for example, that the object before you is to ask for a cup of coffee, it really makes little difference if you say "may I have some coffee?" or "is that coffee I see?" Not that one can go around changing every line in a show, but knowing the meaning of the lines, the key points to be made, the purpose of the scene as it builds from beat to beat is an enormous help in regulating timing. It is also a foolproof way to keep from getting lost or stumbling over a forgotten line.

Good actors find that they automatically begin to analyze scenes for their intent as well as their content as they work on timing. They also find that at times they alter dialogue slightly to help make their timing more natural. A line like "I will not go there today" may, for example, become "I won't go there today" quite by accident simply because the timing seems better with the use of a contration.

There are no rules about this sort of thing. It is only necessary at this point that you be aware of timing; of how theatrical analysis can aid it; of how it helps the integration of characterization with the flow of production; and of how author, director, and actor must work cooperatively to establish it.

Suggested activities

There are hosts of exercises and activities which can sharpen your dramatic performance and evaluation. Some are suggested below.

1.   Being a student of the dramatic arts in the era of celluloid production has to be a tremendous advantage over the past since the great performances preserved on film can be used not only for enjoyment but for education as well. There are hundreds of great film performances to choose from, dozens of great actors. The suggestions below represent only a handful, but they will provide much in terms of characterization analysis. View them and discuss for each the physical dimensions which reveal the psychology of the characters involved.

a.   The film *Separate Tables* (1957) was acclaimed for its acting. Particularly cited were David Niven, Deborah Kerr, and Wendy Hiller. Study and discuss their performances.

b.   Sir Alec Guinness has long been considered one of this century's premiere actors. In *Kind Hearts and Coronets* (1949), he plays eight separate roles. Compare them and discuss his use of physical characterization.

c.   In 1969, *Midnight Cowboy* was hailed by critics for its superb acting. Evaluate the performances of both John Voight and Dustin Hoffman. What physical devices does Hoffman use to mold his character?

2.   Now study the art of characterization in a musical. Evaluate Rex Harrison's performance as Higgins in the film version of *'My Fair Lady.'* Compare it with Robert Preston's Harold Hill in *'The Music Man'* and Yul Brynner's King in *'The King and I.'*

3.   Try the following exercises to help you define a character.

a.   Be an inanimate object. Define your own situation (a tree in a rain storm, a new car at a test drive, etc.) and use every physical device you wish *except* speech.

b.   Be an animal. Again, define your situation but do not speak.

c.   Define two characters in a situation (husband and wife at divorce hearings, father and son at a ball game, etc.). Assign each role to a performer and ad lib the dialogue to a logical conclusion.

   d.   Now choose two characters from an actual musical scene. Analyze the intent of the scene beat by beat. Then improvise the dialogue in character to reveal the meaning of the scene.

   e.   In mime, perform, any simple task (drinking a glass of water, reading the newspaper, etc.). Do it as you yourself would do it. Now do it as another person might do it (a woman, if you are a man; an elderly person, if you are young; a rich person; a poor person; etc.). Now do it as a particular character in a particular show (Fagin, Eliza Doolittle, Harold Hill, etc.). Now do it as that character with the aid of speech. What changed from rendition to rendition?

   f.   From an actual musical, select a character you are playing or would like to play. Write a history of that character covering the five years *before* and *after* the period in which the musical takes place. This will help you determine the change which occurs during the *musical* life of the character.

D. EVALUATING CHOREOGRAPHIC CONCEPT AND PERFORMANCE

The evaluation of dance in a musical production raises two distinct questions: (1) were the dances integrated with the story in a dramatically meaningful way, and (2) in and of themselves, were they well-conceived and well-executed? The first question has more to do with the writing of a musical, and so we will leave it until later in this chapter. The second question relates directly to considerations of performance, and so we will deal with it here.

Appropriateness of style and length. In judging the conceptualization of the dancing in a musical, the first points to consider are those of style and length. If the dances bear little relationship to the atmosphere of the drama, they will be out of character. If they are too long, they will inhibit the flow of the story. If they are too short, they will fragment the pace of the production and fail to realize their purpose.

I once knew a brilliant choreographer who could never come to grips with these principles. There was no end of originality to his work, but much of it was out of place and endlessly long. In a production of *'Oklahoma!,'* for example, the ballet at the close of Act I lasted almost twenty minutes and contained everything from dancing on point to belly dancing. The result was dramatic chaos. The audience became restless and the mood of the Oklahoma territory at the turn of the century was destroyed.

The guidelines for the choreographer in these matters must remain dramatic ones, not ones of pure choreography or, for that matter, aesthetic ego. Just as for the orchestra a musical must never be considered an instrumental concert, so for the dancers it must not become a choreographic display. The orchestra is there to accompany, the dance to embellish. Neither should usurp the flow of dramatic action.

Choreographic realization. Assuming the style of dance is appropriate, that the dances are the right length, and that there are not too many nor too few of them, the next question is "were they well-performed?" Were the dancers in step with the music; were they in step with each other; were they technically up to the demands of the choreography?

In judging these things it is important to remember to consider not only the dancers per se but the movements given to large production numbers and separate songs. The dancers chosen for purely choreographic routines are, after all, specialists. One expects them to be on top of their game from a technical viewpoint. The critical choreographic problems more often than not arise in the staging of troop movement scenes and songs requiring small ensemble motion.

To distinguish between the three categories of choreographic endeavor, let us

73.

consider an example from the literature. In *'Fiddler on the Roof'* the distinctions are clear. The "Wedding Dance" done at the marriage of Tevye's daughter is a dance pure and simple. It has no songs concurrent with it; it has its own music; it is designed to be realized by dancers specialized to the task. The opening number, "Tradition," is quite another story. "Tradition" is a song which introduces virtually every character in the show. It cannot simply be performed in a stagnant tableau from start to finish. It requires movement—the movement of an entire cast. It may employ frozen positions here, coordinated hand gestures there, coordinated walking, even dance steps. All of that is up to the directors in charge of choreography and staging. Whatever is used, however, there will be non-dancers mingled with dancers, and that will present special problems for the choreographer. The song "Matchmaker," sung by Tevye's five daughters, represents the third choreographic genre. Again, the song calls for more than a stationary singing. It is interspersed with dialogue, contains climactic peaks as well as valleys, and needs movement to bring it to life. The waltz tempo of the song lends itself much more to dance steps than the more ponderous duple meter of "Tradition." Therefore, in numbers like "Matchmaker," the choreographer must really create a hybrid between pure song and pure dance.

The evaluation of choreography takes all these things into account. So should the conceptualization of the choreographer. In fact, so must the choice of show and casting process. If they don't, the realization of the choreography hasn't much chance of being good. Again, like so much in the musical theatre, the nature of the pre-production foundation is critical to the performance itself. In choosing *'The Sound of Music,'* one must be aware that there are few troop movement scenes and little dancing. In choosing *'Oliver,'* one must be aware of the large number of troop movement scenes and the demands that they will have upon the cast. In choosing *'A Chorus Line,'* one must know that dancing is nearly everything.

Suggested activities

1. Attend a musical and evaluate the concept and performance of the choreography. What was strong? What was weak? How might it have been improved?

2. If possible, view the motion picture version of *'The Music Man.'* Evaluate the dancing and categorize the numbers as pure dance, troop movement, and song-with-motion. Which number did you find most effective? Which was least effective? Try to back up your answers will well-considered theatrical insight.

3. Choose a pure dance, troop movement scene, or song-with-motion from the literature to choreograph. Consider the limitations of your environment and talent pool, then try to stage an effective rendition of your selection. Note the decisions you make and the reasons for them.

E. EVALUATING THEATRICAL TECHNOLOGY

The evaluation of technology has four aspects: lighting, sound, scenic design, and the performance of various crews. We will consider each in turn.

Lighting. The dramatic focus of a scene, the smooth passage from one scene to another, the creation of mood, the illusion of the passage of time—these are all in large measure the result of the lighting in a musical production. If well-designed, lighting can enhance the pacing and meaning of a show immeasurably; if poorly designed, it can ruin it.

Remember as you judge lighting or make your own lighting plots that you are somewhat at the mercy of factors which may be beyond your control. To a large extent the set design will dictate what you should do, and to an absolute extent the electrical hardware available to you will determine what you are able to supply. This is especially true of modern gadgetry.

Intelligent lighting and the evaluation of it begins by assessing the system itself. As soon as this is done, the strengths and weaknesses of the system should be communicated to the set designer and director so that scenery and blocking can work in harmony with the technical capacity of the theatre. Once this is done, the use of colors, the highlighting of areas, the operation of follow spots, the use of scrims and special effects will all be more rational.

There are no rules for automatic success here. The variations of theatres, sets, and lighting systems are too great for that. Lighting design and execution take not only special expertise but creative insight and intelligent planning as well. All this should be taken into account as you judge the lighting you see.

Sound. What used to reside only with the acoustics of a hall and the delicate judgments of performer and director has in this new age of electronics become a highly specialized, highly technical ingredient of musical theatre. Wired and wireless microphones, amplification and equalization systems, special effects, on-site mixing, prerecorded music, computerized balancing, synthesized sound—the gadgetry fairly tumbles over itself in the theatre of today.

As complex as things are, however, in evaluating or planning the sound system of a musical, a few basic principles remain. Has the system utilized the capacity of the theatre to full advantage? Has it, after all is said and done, achieved the proper balances? If the words are clear, the voices not drowned out by music, the stage free of dead spots, the mix and blend of sounds proportionate to the dramatic intent of the scene, and if every seat in the house is capable of hearing all these things, then the sound technicians have done their job. If not, to the extent of the deficiencies, there are criticisms to make and errors to correct.

Scenic design. The design, construction, and decoration of a set have an enormous impact on the pace and ambiance of a musical production. In judging or planning the set, several things must be considered. Does it allow for the swift changing of scenes? Does it enable every seat in the theatre to enjoy a full, clear view of the action? Does it enhance the lighting and sound, allowing both full play to the extent of their technical capacities? Does it integrate with the mood of the drama? Does it allow for the safe and easy passage of actors? Is it, in and of itself, aesthetically pleasing? Does it fully exploit the hall?

A "yes" answer to each of these questions will bring high marks and the promise of a good production. A "no" answer will leave deficiencies which will have to be addressed and accounted for. Again, there are no rules for sets beyond the considerations above. The variations possible are limitless. The best sets are the ones conceived by a confluence of minds: tech directors, music and drama directors, design artists, choreographers. If each has input into the initial design process, the chances of a workable set are good. If the design is done in a dramatic vacuum, problems will usually arise which create a patchwork quilt of haphazard proportions.

Crews.   The actual functioning of the theatrical technology is the province of the many crews which operate behind the scenes of a production. Was the set well-built? Did the lights and sound work correctly? Were props, costumes, and scenery where they were supposed to be when they were supposed to be there? Were the curtains operated smoothly and on time? All this is up to the crews and the crew chiefs who supervise them. A general rule of thumb in judging or running a crew is that they should neither be seen nor heard. Like ghosts in the night, we should only be aware of the results of their work. To the extent we see that work being done (unless it is deliberately made a part of the action), to that extent the fantasy of the drama is dispelled.

Suggested activities

1.   Attend a musical and evaluate each aspect of its theatrical technology. What about it was strong? What was weak, and what might have been done to correct the weaknesses?

2.   Choose a scene from the literature appropriate to the personnel and theatrical environment in which you find yourself. Then do the following:

   a.   Design a set for the scene.
   b.   Build it and decorate it.
   c.   Prepare and execute a lighting plot for it.
   d.   Install a sound system for it.
   e.   Assign crews to operate the technology as you perform the scene.

All of this will require some specialized supervision and knowledge of construction and electronics. If you need to, consult your theatre library and people skilled in theatrical technology.

F. EVALUATING WARDROBE AND MAKE-UP

The physical accoutrements of costuming and make-up bear directly on the mood of the musical. In some shows they are indispensable to the creation of the locale and historical time in which the action takes place. In other shows they mean considerably less. *'The King and I,'* for example, relies heavily upon costuming and make-up to establish the illusion of Siam, the flavor of the 1860's, and the wealth of the palace in which the drama unfolds. For the *'The Fantasticks,'* costuming is much less important. The time is any time, the place, any place. As long as Matt and Louisa appear to be young, their fathers, older, and El Gallo, dashing and urbane, period costuming and elaborate make-up are unnecessary.

Good wardrobe and make-up design, then, have as their chief goal the establishment of character, place, and time. In evaluating them, this is the primary point to consider. There are others, however. Are costumes and make-up aesthetically pleasing? Do they allow movement? Are they designed well for the actors who actually use them? Are they durable? Are they able to be worn and changed within the dramatic confines of the show? Nothing is more absurd, for example, than to hold up a scene while the lead changes into a stunning five-piece outfit. To ruin pacing for a single costume effect is poor directorial judgment. The aim of the performance is, after all, drama and not a fashion show. Better the costume be three pieces, a touch less stunning, and the action more continuous.

Suggested activities

1.   Select any musical production playing near you and evaluate the wardrobe and make-up. Did they help establish character, place, and time? Were they able to do so without inhibiting the pacing or action of the show?

2.   View the motion picture versions of any or all of the following and discuss the use of wardrobe and make-up: *'My Fair Lady,' 'The Music Man,' 'Oliver.'*

3.   Select a show of your own choosing and discuss the costuming and make-up requirements for it. How would you go about meeting them if you were the producer and wardrobe director? Now, within the confines of your environment, costume one or two characters—perhaps an entire scene. What problems did you encounter? How did you solve them?

G. EVALUATING THE QUALITY OF THE WRITING

Finally, the evaluation of a musical must concern itself with the quality of writing which has produced it. No other single thing so shapes the final product as this. No other single thing is as necessary to the job of critic, performer, or director as the understanding of what makes for good writing.

We will divide our investigation of musical writing into three areas: the writing of the libretto; the composition of the music; and the fashioning of the lyrics. In separating the three, however, one must bear in mind that in performance they are not separate. Indeed, the integration of each with the others is a feature we shall specifically study. The separation here is only a literary and pedagogical tool.

It is also important to note that adherence to the many principles to which we will refer in this segment of the text does not guarantee an excellent musical. Artistic works are rarely written by formula. No matter how many rules or guidelines one follows, the spark of creative individuality cannot be legislated by a textbook. Following good creative practices only enhances the opportunity for good musical theatre; it does not in and of itself assure it.

Twelve signs of a good libretto. Take away the music. Remove the lyrics. Eliminate the dancing. Strip your musical of all its technical gadgetry and glittering costumes. What you now have left is a libretto of purely dramatic proportions. You have dialogue, plot, theme, characters—and if they are not valid, believable, moving in and of themselves, nothing you add back will be of literary use.

A libretto must be able to stand on its own as a coherent, well-crafted literary work for a musical to be truly excellent. The addition of music, dancing, lyrics, and production hoopla to a poor libretto merely camouflages the inadequacy of the writing. It does not rectify it, and it cannot compensate for any resultant problems.

Exactly what makes for a better-crafted libretto is the subject of the following pages, and we shall investigate the key ingredients one by one.

1. *Universality of theme.* In literature, people rarely respond to things with which they cannot identify. Maybe they've never been to the location of the story. Maybe they've never experienced the actual events of the story. But somewhere—in the meaning of the events, the unfolding of the relationships, the emotions experienced by the characters—the viewer has to say, "Yes. I've known that. I've felt that. I can empathize with that." If a writer wishes his audience to care about and respond to what is being written, he must touch a human string which vibrates in common, universally, among people.

Let us consider an example we have viewed before, *'Fiddler on the Roof.'* The show is set in the poor village of Anatevka, Russia in the early 1900's on the eve of the Revolution. It shows the effect of the changing times on the Jews of Anatevka, particularly the family of Tevye, the milkman, his wife, and five daughters. It reveals the bigotry of Czarist Russia against the Jews, and the way in which evolving social forces gradually destroy the traditions of Anatevka. In the end, the village itself is abandoned as the Jews are forced to flee from persecution. Families are torn apart, people are imprisoned, life is turned upside down.

'*Fiddler*' opened in 1964, and there were precious few in the millions who saw it who had ever been to Russia or were even alive in the early 1900's. It was hailed by people of every religion, not just Jews. It was applauded by every race, every color. And why? Because all of us are inevitably swept up in the storms of changing times. Change is a constant of human history, and when it is violent, it disassociates whole societies. None of us escapes the incessant reshaping of our lives, and therefore none of us is untouched by the themes of '*Fiddler*' whether or not we are Jewish refugees from Czarist Russia.

Who in the audiences of 1964 and afterward has not known the problems of Tevye? The refugees of World War II, of Korea, of Vietnam—they were all Tevye in one way or another. And so were their families and friends. What home in the post-World War II era has not experienced conflict between the traditions of Mama and Papa and the new ways of their children? Racially mixed marriages, new forms of court-ship and sexual expression swept the world in the 1960's—and to some extent have always been a part of the tension between young and old. So when Chava, Tevye's daughter, cries out for her Papa to accept her choice of a gentile husband, she cries out for every young person who fails to meet parental expectations. And when Tevye's heart is broken by that failure, he embodies all parents who cannot reconcile their own wishes with those of their children.

Compare the universal appeal of '*Fiddler*' with a show of considerably less thematic stature, Cole Porter's '*Anything Goes.*' The story concerns a nightclub singer, Reno Sweeney, in love with a wealthy sophisticate, Billy Crocker, who is himself in love with socialite Hope Harcourt. Reno and Hope are both booked on a luxury liner bound from New York to London. Billy, in an effort to pursue Hope, buys a ticket for the trip from an escaped criminal (Public Enemy #13) posing as the Reverend Dr. Moon. Moon has been saving the ticket for a partner who has failed to show up. Crocker disguises himself as the partner in order to keep from being thrown off the ship as a stowaway.

The ship sails with Billy now trying to pass as Moon's assistant, now trying to win Hope's heart. Reno pines away for Billy, and Dr. Moon continues to try to avoid discovery. Eventually, Moon is discovered and thrown in the brig. The Captain then holds a revival meeting to save Moon's soul.

When the ship docks, Hope is thrust into a marriage of financial convenience with Sir Evelyn Oakleigh. At the last minute, a turn of financial fortune frees her to pursue Billy. Sir Evelyn at this point becomes attracted to Reno, and Moon is released when a late-arriving FBI report declares him harmless.

Even a casual synopsis of Porter's plot cannot disguise its limited appeal. The characters and situations are frothy fantasy with little rhyme or reason. Nothing they do and very little they feel are common to the average audience member, and in the end, the plot is more silly than universal. But there is something even more at fault than the lack of universality and that is the lack of thematic focus.

2. *Thematic focus.* When the events and ideas of a literary work are poorly integrated, when they do not bear a direct relationship to each other, when things occur for illogical reasons or no reasons at all, the work is said to lack thematic focus.

And poor thematic focus weakens a work for two very important reasons. First, it fragments the attention of the onlooker by constantly shifting from one point to another. It is like trying to eat more than one meal at a time. The palate can't take the juxtaposition of two unrelated dishes. No matter how enticing each may be, they end in a gluttonous conflict which renders both unenjoyable. Second, a string of unintegrated events leads to an arbitrariness which destroys the effect of representational theatre because it taxes the credibility of the onlooker. Again, let us return to *'Anything Goes'* by way of illustration.

In Porter's work, we really have several stories being told at once. There is the Reno-Billy story which, though it opens the show, quickly dies away in favor of the Billy-Hope story. To this is added the saga of Dr. Moon who has little to do with either Reno or Hope. Finally, at practically the end of the show, we have the Hope-Sir Evelyn story which conveniently changes into a Reno-Sir Evelyn relationship, neither of which has anything to do with the saga of Dr. Moon. In a melange of plots like this, a whole host of questions must ultimately arise in the mind of the literary analyst. Who is the central character—Reno, Billy or Dr. Moon? Why is there no developed relationship between Reno and Hope? They are, after all, involved with the same man. What connection exists between Dr. Moon and Crocker's women? Why does the Captain feel compelled to hold a revival meeting? Why is Sir Evelyn, whose purpose in wanting to marry Hope is central to the Billy-Hope conflict, not important to the show until the end of it? Why is Dr. Moon, portrayed from the beginning as an escaped felon, ultimately called "harmless" by the FBI and released?

One can rationalize a series of answers to these questions but none of them will have the stamp of reality. In real life, the FBI doesn't arbitrarily drop people from the "most wanted list" because they are "harmless." If they were that harmless, what would they be doing on the list to begin with? Sea captains do not hold revival meetings in mid-passage. People do not fall in and out of love at a moment's notice as Reno and Sir Evelyn seem to do.

So what, you argue? So the plot doesn't mirror reality. Why should it? Because it is representational theatre. *'Anything Goes'* is not written in the mold of *'The Fantasticks'* or the fantasy of a fairy tale. When Cinderella wishes to go to the ball, we accept the fact that her fairy godmother can turn a pumpkin into a coach because from the outset we have been told by the genre of the writing to suspend our expectations of reality. Fantasy is the game, and we agree to abide by its rules. So, too, in allegorical theatre. When El Gallo turns from the events of the drama to address the audience directly, we accept it because we have agreed to play the game of story theatre. *'Anything Goes'* chooses the game of representational theatre, and so it must do things for reasons which mirror reality. When it does not, it becomes literarily inconsistent.

Compare the poor thematic focus of Porter's work to *'Fiddler.'* Here we have a clearly defined central character, Tevye, to whom every other character relates directly. Do we have several love stories? Yes: Tevye and his wife, Golde; Tevye's daughter, Tzeitel, and Motel, the tailor; Tevye's daughter, Hodel, and Perchik, the student; Tevye's daughter, Chava, and Fyedka, the Russian gentile. But see how each relates to Tevye and how each reveals the dissolution of Tevye's world because it exemplifies the growing social and political unrest of Tevye's times. The integration of events is bound to a single theme; the logic of events is acceptable because it is the logic of reality.

At this point a defender of *'Anything Goes'* (and shows of similar ilk) might argue, "So what? So the writing is inconsistent. The musical was a big hit. Audiences loved it. It made lots of money. It had great songs. What difference did the writing make?" To which I answer, for people who do not care about good writing, no difference. Mediocrity and escapist theatre have always had their place and, for those inclined to enjoy them, probably always will. However, the aim of this text is not the fostering of mediocre theatre. In fact, we have already seen that an abundance of it is swiftly putting an end to Broadway because mediocrity cannt flower forever. It hasn't the staying power. One educates a doctor, hopefully, to be a good one; a chef, to make good meals; an engineer, to build things which will last. So, too, one educates people to produce good theatre.

3. *Theatrical profundity.* The themes of a musical can be both universal and focused and yet still achieve less than their fullest potential. To realize that potential they must rise above the level of banality to deal with issues that are profound. Consistently, we find such thematic profundity in works which draw upon historical and social forces. Consider the following examples.

Love between a man and a woman is certainly a universal theme, and if handled properly it can certainly be focused. Yet the history of Broadway musicals fairly overflows with the love story formula "boy meets girl, boy loses girl, boy finds girl." We see it in shows like *'The Pajama Game,' 'Guys and Dolls,' 'Annie Get Your Gun,' 'Brigadoon,'* and countless others where the romance never seems to rise above the level of the commonplace.

Now consider *'My Fair Lady,' 'West Side Story,'* and *'The King and I,'* all romances but with far more profound themes. 'Fair Lady' sets its story against the rigid class system of Britain and in doing so shows the effect that social forces have on people's feelings for each other. *'West Side Story'* explores the tragic consequences which bigotry has on love. *'The King and I'* develops its story in relationship to the issues of slavery, women's rights, and international politics. It shows how the love between people can be distorted by forces beyond their relationships. In each of these three musicals, formulas are replaced with themes of deep human significance, and in two of them—*'West Side Story'* and *'The King and I'*—the romances are never realized because the forces are sufficient to destroy them.

The greatest musical libretti, then, have themes which are not only universal and sharply focused but profound as well.

4. *Clearly defined conflict.* There are few things in literature which help to establish the thematic focus of a work or give it architectural impetus more than the early and clear statement of a conflict. Conflict is the fuel which drives dramatic motion, giving intent and direction to the plot. Without conflict, there is little chance for the development of ideas, events, or characters. If there is no conflict, there is usually no reason to tell the story, no interest, no chance for the exposition and resolution of tension. To use a crude analogy, conflict is the current which keeps the river moving. In its absence the river turns into a lake and the transportation of the audience becomes impossible.

To have conflict one must have forces in opposition to each other. These are commonly known as protagonist and antagonist. Narrowly defined, the protagonist is the central character, the person who espouses a cause or takes a stand. The antagonist is the character who opposes that stand and acts as an adversary. More broadly defined, the protagonist is the force which initiates the action while the antagonist is the force which resists the action. Tevye is the protagonist of *'Fiddler.'* He wishes to preserve his traditions and embarks upon those courses of action (like arranging the marriage of his daughter to the town butcher) which will accomplish his aims. The antagonist of *'Fiddler'* is actually not one person but the spirit of change embodied in all those who stand opposed to Tevye's traditions. Perchik, the rebellious student; Chava, the daughter who marries outside the faith; th Russian Constable who must persecute the Jews of Anatevka at the behest of the Czar; they are all the antagonist.

Analyses of dramatic conflict can become very complex. For instance, it is possible in *'Fiddler'* to make the case that the protagonist is the tide of social change itself, while Tevye is the antagonist who resists that change. Whichever analysis one accepts, the literary point remains the same. Conflict must involve opposing forces, and in order to be meaningful dramatically, it must be stated clearly and early in the game.

5. *Architectural awareness.* We have already discussed the awareness of architecture from the point of view of performer and director. It is even more critical for the writer to bear in mind. The sculpture of beats to make a scene and scenes to make a show is an essential ingredient because it gives shape and direction to the unfolding of plot and theme.

In architecting his writing, the author must bear three critical needs in mind: he needs to avoid extraneous material, to allow for a variety of moods, and to juxtapose material so that the drama has contrasting moments. The reasons for this are fairly obvious. Extraneous material, that is, dialogue or action which neither advances the plot nor develops theme and character, is merely a waste of theatrical time, and time is the indispensable environment in which drama occurs. The lack of contrast and variety renders architectural motion impossible because it keeps everything on the same emotional level. Let us consider some examples.

In Act I, Scene 8 of *'The Pajama Game,'* hero Sid, manager of the pajama factory, and heroine Babe, one of the leaders of the pajama workers' union, have a talk. They are falling in love but sense that there will be trouble ahead for their romance because they are on opposite sides of a growing labor/management conflict. The conflict, in fact, erupts, and by the end of Act I, we can clearly see that it has, indeed, taken a personal toll on our leading couple. Then in Act II, Scene 2, Sid and Babe meet again, duplicating virtually the conversation they had in Act I. The second conversation isn't dramatically necessary. We already know they are in love. We have already seen that their romance is being jeopardized by company politics. Rehashing past events at this point simply wastes time and delays the progress of the plot. The general literary rule of thumb here is "don't tell the audience what it already knows."

Now consider the cases of variety and contrast. Perhaps the best model ever written in this regard is *'West Side Story,'* the emotional reworking of *Romeo and Juliet*, set in the slums of Manhattan. Librettist Arthur Laurents does a masterful job juxtaposing scenes of tenderness, tragedy, and comedy in a progression of events which is never stagnant or repetitive. The opening scenes of Act II are an excellent illustration of his technique as a literary craftsman. Act I has ended with a gang war between the Jets and the Sharks in which Tony, the white leader of the Jets, has killed Bernardo, the Puerto Rican leader of the Sharks, even though Tony is deeply in love with Maria, Bernardo's sister. The impact of the end of Act I is profoundly tragic. But now, how does Laurents open Act II? With a light, comic scene between Maria and her friends who are unmindful of the murder of Bernardo and who are busily engaged in admiring themselves (the song "I Feel Pretty"). The juxtaposing of moods is brilliant. By not allowing the audience to dwell on the tragedy, the tragedy is made all the more real because it never degenerates into heavy-handed restatement.

Laurents continues to maintain variety and contrast throughout the musical. The lighthearted opening of Act II is followed by a scene of incredible tenderness in which Tony seeks Maria's understanding and both dream of a world cleansed of racial hatred ("Somewhere"). This, in turn, is followed by the comic relief of the Jets mimicking the New York police ("Officer Krupke").

In the hands of a literary technician like Laurents, it is really impossible to have a dull moment. The action is always being propelled forward; the mood is never stagnant. When one analyzes the craft of the libretto, it is not hard to understand why *'West Side Story'* is a classic.

6. *Integration of humor, tragedy, song, and dance with plot.* In good writing nothing happens by accident. Characters change for a reason. Circumstances develop because an inevitable logic causes them to evolve that way. Humor and tragedy, song and dance grow out of the events at hand; they are not superimposed upon those events. There is, in short, an integration of elements which binds the work into an organically unified statement.

The opposite of the integrated style of the literary craftsman is the "deus ex machina" style of a poorer writer. The phrase "deus ex machina" (literally translated from Latin as "God out of a machine") was used in Greek theatre to refer to a god who would arbitrarily untangle the loose ends of a plot. In time it has come to stand for any artificial contrivance used to resolve dramatic weaknesses which are not resolved through the logical flow of the drama itself.

Libretti which rely on "deus ex machina" rather than integration are bound to be weak because they abandon the dramatic logic upon which they are based and thus become internally inconsistent. The inconsistency, in turn, erodes the believability of the story and thus renders it far less emotionally satisfying to the audience.

Consider, for example, how absurd it would be if at the end of *'West Side Story'* a magic fairy would automatically appear, wave a wand, and cause Tony to rise from the dead and take Maria in his arms to live happily ever after. The whole impact of *'West Side Story'* rests on the fact that the love between Tony and Maria is destroyed by the racial prejudice which kills him. Bring him to life at the hands of an imposed savior, and the tragedy becomes illogical, indeed, almost comical.

This is a rather extreme example of what a poorly integrated plot would look like, but there are others from the actual literature. Let's take a look at them and at some examples of well-integrated writing.

In *'Guys and Dolls'* the secondary romance between Adelaide and Nathan is stormy from the very outset of the plot. Adelaide wants to get married; Nathan does not. Literally nothing happens to change either character through the entirety of the show; yet at the very end, in an effort to pull the "happy ending rabbit" out of a theatrical hat, Nathan relents and agrees to be wed. There is no reason for his change of heart. It is never preceded by a dramatic set-up. He never even talks about it with

Adelaide in a way which would lead one to believe he is mellowing toward matrimony. So when he decides to take the plunge, we really can't believe it, and because it is hard to believe, it is hard to feel anything deep about it. The "deus ex machina" of wedlock is more a literary obligation than a dramatic release. It is like the checkout clerk who is obliged to say "have a nice day" as you hand over your money. The thought is insincere.

In *'The Pajama Game,'* the union meeting at which the factory workers plan their strategy is concluded by a big dance number, "Steam Heat." The number has absolutely no relevance to the motion of the story. In fact, it is introduced by the union President as a kind of afterthought to the meeting. "Before you go," he says, "Gladys and some of the boys have put together a little entertainment." One suspects the number was inserted into the show to highlight Carol Haney, the dancer who played Gladys, or to assuage a backer or producer who wanted to see a dance somewhere in the production.

The imposition of numbers on a libretto can only retard its progress, and a sure way to spot them is simply to ask the following question: if they were omitted from the show, would the meaning of the scene or the production change substantially? In the cases above, not a thing would turn out differently if "Steam Heat" weren't danced or Adelaide never married Nathan.

All of which is not to say that Carol Haney shouldn't have danced or that, taken alone, "Steam Heat" isn't a cute number. But the money of a backer, the aggrandizement of a producer, and the exploitation of a talented performer can never become the literary justification of a good writer.

Now consider another musical marriage, that of Chava to Fyedka which we have discussed earlier. Here the decision to wed is not sudden nor is it irrelevant to the flow of events. It is prepared and made part of the thematic exposition of *'Fiddler'* because it represents yet one more instance in which Tevye's beloved traditions and family are destroyed. It is wedlock integrated to theme.

Finally, compare the "Steam Heat" scene with the dance from *'Gypsy'* entitled "All I Need Is the Girl." We are in the alley behind a theatre. Louise, the no-talent sister of star Dainty June, is listening to Tulsa, June's dancing partner, planning his future act. As Tulsa explains it to her, he begins to dance it out in reality, using Louise as his trial partner. Although Louise knows it is June he has in mind, for the moment she becomes the star and Tulsa, her handsome beau. The dance is inextricably bound to the development of Louise's character and the realization of Tulsa's dreams. Later, when Tulsa runs off with June and Louise does become a star, we see how important this scene really is.

"All I Need Is the Girl" doesn't work because some producer said to Jule Styne, "Hey, put a dance in Act II," nor does it work because Paul Wallace (the original Tulsa) asked for a number to show off his skills. It works because it is more than just a dance, because it is a part of the plot which furthers the development of two key characters. Take it out of the show, and Louise never has the impetus to develop the positive self-image which ultimately makes her a star able to escape the clutches of an emotionally abusive stage mother.

7. *Dimensional and consistent characterization.* We have already discussed the importance of dimensional characterization to the actor involved in representational theatre and archetype characterization to the actor involved in allegorical theatre.

Without belaboring the topic, it is the writer who must provide the actor with the material on which those characterizations can be built. The important thing for the writer to remember is that, once the nature of the characterization is chosen, it should remain consistent throughout the musical. El Gallo, for example, cannot suddenly convert from omniscient narrator in an allegorical libretto to dimensional villain in a representational drama. That would not only destroy his own credibility but the credibility of the entire play. He may grow; he may change; but he must do so within the confines of the literary style in which he has been created.

8. *Believable comedy and tragedy.* There are few literary ingredients handled as poorly as comedy and tragedy, not simply because writers insist on imposing them upon situations to which they are not indigenous, but also because many writers do not understand what makes them believable. Strange as it may seem, what makes them believable is the presence of a contrary or opposite condition.

"Show me a man in trouble, and I'll show you a funny man," the old saying goes. Every comedian worth his salt knows it to be true. The premise of comedy is its opposite. The person in trouble who perceives his problem in exaggerated terms and tries to remedy it with exaggerated means will always produce comedy. Yes, the exaggerations are necessary also, but they can only come after the trouble has been exposed.

Consider, for a moment, the comedy of Charlie Chaplin, generally regarded as a genius in the field. Along comes his Little Tramp, blithely flirting with a pretty woman. They pass beneath a construction ladder on which her husband is working as a mason. The husband spies Charlie's advances, and as Charlie obliviously continues his flirtation, the husband drops a brick on his head. We laugh. Charlie looks up, trying to find the cause of his problems. His view is hidden by the construction scaffolding. He shrugs and makes another advance toward the pretty woman. Pow—another brick. We laugh again. Charlie holds his hand out as if to check for rain. He unfolds the umbrella he carries lest another "hailstone" strike. A third time he cozies up to the woman. Bang—a third brick right through the umbrella. And so it goes.

Chaplin makes us laugh both because his pain is real and because his remedy for it is nonsensical. The premise of the bit is a real conflict between Charlie and the husband. The bricks are really thrown. They really knock him down. Without that element of trouble, Charlie's reaction—also necessary to the comedy—would not be possible.

Now consider the wonderfully crafted comedy of *'Fiddler.'* Act I ends with the wedding of Tevye's daughter being destroyed by the Czar's soldiers. People are beaten, the merriment is ended. We do not laugh as the curtain closes. But Act II begins some months later with Tevye talking to God as he pulls his milk cart along. "That was some dowry you gave my daughter," he says, and then continues by asking God to mend his horse's leg so that he will be relieved of the burden of pulling the cart. The speech gets laughs because Tevye's troubles are real, integral to the drama, and he makes light of them. His reaction is also necessary to produce our laughter, but again, without the troubles there would be no reaction.

What applies to comedy, a unity of opposite theatrical moods, also applies to the presentation of believable tragedy. Consider how Dickens treats the end of *A Tale of Two Cities*, one of the greatest novels ever written. Sidney Carton, a drunk who has squandered his talents on frivolous pursuits, has decided to give his life to save the husband of the woman he has secretly loved. He contrives to exchange places with the husband in a French jail on the eve of the husband's execution. But now, rather then bemoaning his fate, Dickens has him write one of the most moving letters in all literature. "Do not pity me," Carton writes to Lucy, "for I see that I will hold a sanctuary in the hearts of those I love for what I do." Carton looks upon his death as the best thing he has ever done, and because he sees it as an ennobling act, a positive, wonderful thing, we feel it with an even deeper sense of tragedy.

In the musical theatre, both *'Fiddler'* and *'West Side Story'* use the same technique. Tevye's world is shattered, yet as he leaves his home, he walks proudly and proclaims confidence in the future. Tony dies in Maria's arms still declaring his love and still clinging to the hope that they will find a place to be happy together. And after he dies, the warring gangs are united. The curtain falls not upon them fighting or crying over Tony but upon them walking together in greater understanding. The tragedies are intensified because the characters to whom they occur are able to look beyond them to a positive, almost redemptive resolution of conflict.

9. *Showing rather than telling.* The essential difference between the stage and screen on the one hand, and the novel on the other, is that the former can visualize while the latter can only describe. In order to utilize the medium of theatre to its fullest advantage, then, it is incumbent upon the writer to communicate the flow of events through the action of characters rather than through simple explanatory dialogue, at least as much as possible. Let's consider an example.

Suppose *'My Fair Lady'* were a novel. It would be very convenient and entirely appropriate to the literary medium to reveal a growing relationship between Higgins and Eliza in a paragraph (or page or chapter, depending upon the detail involved) of expository description. "During the next few months," the book might go, "Higgins and Eliza worked round the clock. Mercilessly, he drove her on toward the goal of proper speech—he insisting, she obedient, even through her anger."

In the musical, we can—and must—bring those months to life, and fortunately we have two craftsmen (Shaw and Alan Jay Lerner) who know that very well. The result is Act I, Scene 6 of *'My Fair Lady,'* the time-passage scene in which we see Eliza's struggle to master the English language, the scene which finally erupts in the triumphant song "The Rain in Spain."

Because the medium is visual, we need not be *told* that Higgins is a tyrant; we can *see* him being a tyrant. We can *see* Eliza bristling with anger, and we can *see* the two of them rejoice in her conquest of the spoken word. How much duller, how much less skillful a use of the medium it would have been to have omitted the visualization of Eliza's metamorphosis. It could have been done through expository dialogue. The months might have passed *between* Act I, Scene 5 and Act I, Scene 6. Scene 6 could have begun with Higgins saying to his friend Pickering, "You know, Pickering, I've been working with Eliza for three months now, and I've driven her like a tyrant. I know she hates me for it, but last night I finally got her to say 'the rain in Spain stays mainly on the plain' correctly." Thank goodness in this case both Shaw and Lerner had the craftsmanship to know better.

By the way, the "show, don't tell" rule of thumb is also appropriate in the novel. Even when limited to narrative and dialogue alone, it is possible to manipulate them so that the exposition of ideas and the development of characters are revealed in more clever and dramatic ways than overt explanation. To use an example we touched upon previously, it is much more powerful for Dickens to *show* how deeply Carton loves Lucy by having him die to save her husband than it would be for him to *tell* us in written narrative, "Over the years, Carton fell deeply in love with Lucy Manette."

10. *Avoiding expository explanation.* All events are part of a continuum. Stories reveal only a section of that continuum. Presumably, events went on before the action begins which brought it to the stage at which we discover it. Presumably, events will continue after the story at hand is over. Eliza, for example, was a lower class flower girl for many years before we encounter her outside Covent Gardens in the opening scene of *'My Fair Lady,'* and she and Higgins will continue their relationship for many years after the final curtain.

To the extent that the knowledge of past events is necessary to the understanding of present action, writers must find a way to reveal them to the audience. If the revelation occurs through deliberate expository explanation, however, the actions of the present are stopped, and the audience becomes quickly bored. In good writing, audiences are thrown into the dramatic situation from the opening moment. They are then filled in on past events of importance bit by bit as the writing unfolds. Expository explanation is skillfully intertwined with the action of the drama so that the understanding of the past is not accomplished at the expense of involvement with the present.

Consider a really beautiful example of the "leap in and catch up later" rule of thumb from *'The King and I.'* When we first meet Anna we know very little about her. We see her ready to debark her ship in Siam, frightened and alone in a strange land. We don't know why she is there or what in her past has driven her from England to this distant Asian shore. It might have been easy for Oscar Hammerstein to tell us then and there, but he doesn't. The ship captain could conveniently have said to her, "I'm not sure it was wise for you to leave England so soon after your husband's death. What do you expect to find in Siam?" And Anna might easily have answered, "Escape from the past, Captain, and a chance to fill the void by finding a purpose as the tutor to the King's children."

What we get instead is action to replace expository explanation. Baggage is unloaded. An ominous landing party is sent to fetch Anna to the palace. The song "Whistle a Happy Tune" is sung to bolster Anna's courage. We are thrust into the events of the moment. Our dramatic river is given its current, and we have no choice but to be swept downstream by it. When *is* the past revealed? Later, when the revelation can integrate with the action—when Anna meets and befriends the young Tuptim. Tuptim asks for advice in her clandestine love affair with Lun Tha, and Anna answers by telling her about Tom, the man she has loved and lost. When Anna sings "Hello, Young Lovers," she not only captivates us with the moment, she fills us in on her past, and we understand in so much more dramatically meaningful ways why she has come to Siam.

11. *Using dramatic "hooks."* The opening of *'The King and I'* illustrates another important sign of good writing, the use of the dramatic "hook." A hook is something which intrigues the audience, involves it, and drives it to ask for more. In the example above, the hook is the withholding of information. We are thrust into a situation the details of which we don't understand. Our natural reaction (and the one Mr. Hammerstein was deliberately provoking) is to ask, "Why are we in Siam? What is Anna up to? What is her relationship to the King?" All of which leads to

the inevitable question, "What will happen next?" If a writer cannot get his audience to ask that question, he has lost them.

In the conventional two-act structure of the American musical, there are three places where dramatic hooks are indispensable: the first scene of Act I, the last scene of Act I, and the final scene of the show. The hook in Act I, Scene I is necessary to involve the audience immediately. The hook in the last scene of Act I is necessary to bring the audience back from intermission. The hook at the end of the production is needed to build the drama to an emotional climax which will send the audience out of the theatre satisfied.

By way of example, let us again turn to '*Fiddler,*' one of the best-crafted libretti in the history of the American musical. Act I opens with Tevye's Prologue and the ensemble singing "Tradition." Because the dramatic genre is story theatre and because we are thrust into the panoply of an entire village, we cannot help becoming involved. The style of writing and grandeur of production hook us like fish in a barrel. Act I ends with the destruction of Tzeitel's wedding. As the curtain closes, we cannot fail to ask ourselves, "What is going to happen to the Jews of Anatevka?" We are fairly compelled to return after intermission to find out. Finally, as the last scene ends, because the tragedy has been well-crafted, we leave the theatre moved by the suffering, heroism, stoicism, and optimism of Tevye and his people. We cannot fail to care for them, to identify with them, and to make them a part of our literary lives forever.

12. *Consistency of viewpoint.* Stories can be told and action unfolded in a variety of literary styles. From the point of view of time, writers can use present, past, and future tenses and whole ranges like perfect, imperfect, subjective, etc., besides. From the point of view of person, writers can choose between the first person "I," second person "you," or third person "he, she, it" in either singular or plural form. From the point of view of literary perspective, a writer can relate action from the vantage point of a central character, a peripheral character, an objective observer not directly related to the action, or an omniscient almost god-like posture. Finally, all these elements can be combined in countless ways.

"Call me Ismael," *Moby Dick* begins, and Herman Melville draws us into history with the first person present tense narrative of a peripheral (albeit important) character. "It was the best of times; it was the worst of times," writes Dickens in the opening lines of *A Tale of Two Cities.* His view is third person, past tense, and omniscient.

Every view carries with it a certain flavor and provides the author certain latitudes as well as certain restrictions. For example, general expository commentary on the world is a bit easier from the omniscient view than from the view of a specific character—or if not easier, then at least more direct. If Ismael knows nothing about education, for example, Melville cannot have him wax poetic on the subject. If Melville narrates his story from the omniscient view of a commentator, he can conveniently wax poetic on anything.

The flavor of a literary work is greatly shaped by the writer's choice of viewpoint. Let's consider an example. Our story deals with, say, a British scouting patrol in the jungles of Burma during World War II. Our protagonist is the patrol leader. If we tell our story first person, past, central, it might begin like this: "I got up at dawn and shook the rest of my men awake. I knew our patrol wouldn't be easy. The sooner we got started, the better." Now consider it as an objective narrative in the present tense. "6:25 A.M. Sargeant Evans rises. He wakes his men and heads out on patrol." There is quite a difference in the mood created for the reader.

The literary point to be made here is that in good writing the view is consistent— consistently applied, consistent with the nature of the theme, consistent with the action, consistent with the characters. Story theatre, for example, is ideally suited to allegorical drama because in allegory the view is often omniscient and the characters often objective. Consider the use of El Gallo in *'The Fantasticks.'* Louisa, the teenage heroine, fantasizes to the audience, "The moon turns red on my birthday every year, and it always will until somebody saves me and takes me back to my palace." At which point, El Gallo turns to the audience. "That is a typical remark," he says. "The other symptoms vary. She thinks that she's a princess; that her name must be in French or sometimes Eurasian, although she isn't sure what that is."

What an integrated blend of theme and literary viewpoint. The play deals with overdrawn archetype characters, Louisa's being the typical adolescent female drawn into the hormonal posturing of romantic fantasy. The viewpoint (omniscient, present) of El Gallo is perfect to allow him to comment upon her. The juxtaposing of the two produces a kind of humor and dramatic ambiance which has made *'The Fantasticks'* a classic.

Suggested activities

1.   There have been those who have suggested that the King's death in *'The King and I'* is a "deus ex machina" designed to produce a last-minute air of tragedy. Do you agree with this assessment? If so, what might you do as a writer to better integrate his death with the story? If you don't agree, why not?

2.   There have been those who have suggested that the hook at the end of Act I of *'The Sound of Music'* is poorly placed. Why do you think this criticism has been voiced? Do you agree or disagree with it? If you agree, how might the problem be remedied?

3.   Choose one musical from the list below and analyze its treatment of each of the twelve signs of a good libretto: *'The Music Man,' 'The Fantasticks,' 'South Pacific,' 'Fiddler on the Roof,' 'West Side Story,' 'The King and I,' 'Gypsy.'*

Ten signs of good composition.   As we have noted before, a text of this kind cannot teach the technical aspects of each specialized skill needed to create a musical. How to dance, compose music, build a set, operate a lighting board, etc., are long and detailed studies requiring many texts of their own. For the purposes of the stage performer, writer, director, and producer reading here, we can only treat these subjects in a general way. It is in this manner that we will investigate the elements of musical craftsmanship.

1.   *Using musical tension-release mechanisms to architect composition.*   The architecture of music is no less crucial to its crafting than the architecture of the libretto, and we can chart musical architecture in much the same way we charted literary architecture by using a time/emotion pictograph. Music which has shapes which are neither schizophrenic wobblings from high emotional peaks to low valleys nor sta-

tionary lines showing little if any movement will exhibit a higher degree of architectural craftsmanship.

As a student of the musical theatre, it behooves you to know why an architectural graph will rise and fall. Generally speaking, it is because elements are being employed which either increase or decrease musical tension. Below, in layman's terms, we will enumerate some of the more important compositional elements used to create the tensions which sculpt sound emotionally.

Harmonic dissonance. Sounds which are harsh or grating to the audience are called dissonances. Sounds which are perceived as pleasant are called consonances. Dissonances increase musical tension in much the same way that spices add zest to food. Consonances, on the other hand, tend to resolve tension.

Increased rhythmic activity. Tempo, meter, and the placement of syncopations (unusual accents) all contribute to the rhythmic flow of music. Faster tempi, more complex meters, and frequent syncopation tend to increase tension.

Dynamic extremes. Dynamics in music refer to the use of louds and softs. In general, extremes of dynamics tend to produce tension much as they do in speech. A shout or a whisper will raise an eyebrow much quicker than a normal speaking tone. Louder volumes and levels of sound which crescendo from soft to loud are particularly good at increasing musical tension.

Registral extremes. As with the human reaction to temperature where very high and very low create physical tension, very high and very low pitches also create tension. Centralized registers (i.e., pitches which are neither high nor low) tend to reduce musical tension.

Disjunct motion. Music which leaps about with great intervallic distances between pitches will produce much more tension than musical lines which are made up of tones not widely separated. This is especially true if the disjunct tones are articulated in short, staccato rhythms as opposed to long, legato note values.

Textural thickness. In musical terms, texture refers to the number of separate musical parts being sounded at any given time. A flute playing alone, for example, produces one-part texture. One hundred flutes all playing the same part also produce one-part texture. However, two flutes, each playing a separate part, produce two-part texture. The thicker the texture (that is, the more separate parts being played at any time), the more the musical tension.

It is easy to see how these six basic musical elements work to help sculpt the sound into architectural peaks and valleys. Consider the "Dance at the Gym" from 'West Side Story' by Leonard Bernstein. The music has two greatly contrasting sections, the "Mambo" which simulates the war between the Jets and the Sharks, and the "Cha-Cha" which depicts the moment when Tony and Maria meet. The emotional pitch of the Mambo is extremely high. Its tempo is fast; its sonorities are filled with dissonance. Musical lines leap about frantically in an atmosphere of thick orchestrations and loud volume levels. Then, as Tony and Maria draw toward each other, Bernstein slows the tempo to, as the musical directions describe, a "delicate cha-cha." The volume drops; the orchestration thins; the melodic line becomes smooth, consonant, quiet.

Bernstein is generally regarded as a master composer in the musical theatre, not only because of the way he uses musical devices to build beautifully architected works, but also because he is a sophisticated craftsman of melodic construction, form, orchestration, and the use of harmony and counterpoint—all of which we will discuss briefly below. Bernstein stands as an exception to much in the American musical. It is universally acknowledged as a sad but true fact that, in comparison with the great operatic and concert composers of the so-called "classical" world, composers of musicals lag far behind in knowledge and skill. Perhaps one day, as the audiences of musical theatre become more discriminating and its composers more astute, that will change.

2. *Melodic crafting.* The composition of melody is a fundamental skill which has been taught for many centuries. The best melodies are those which show a consistent application of the tonality from which they are made and an architecture which allows for the establishment and resolution of tension. Richard Rodgers's "You'll Never Walk Alone" from *'Carousel'* is the prototype of a well-crafted melody. It consistently utilizes the major-minor scale system and is architected so that it rises inexorably from a calm, quiet start to a truly moving climactic end.

3. *Inventive use of harmony.* All music is organized around systems of pitches which act as the underlying skeleton of melody and harmony. Those systems have evolved over time so that the works of different centuries or geographical regions have different styles, much as the styles of dress or food or architecture vary from place to place and era to era. Chinese music sounds as it does because it employs a pitch system (the pentatonic scale) which gives its melodies and harmonies a distinctive flavor. The modal scales of the Middle Ages and Renaissance were responsible for the character of the music of those times, etc.

In the twentieth century, there are many pitch systems which can be employed: the major-minor diatonic scale system, the major-minor system modified by chromatic alteration, the whole-tone scale system, systems of polytonality, the system of atonality, the system of serial atonality—to name just a few. The technical definition of these ways of organizing pitches is beyond the scope of this text. However, it is important to know that never before this century have so many systems and styles been in vogue at one time. Never before has the composer had so great a choice of colors on his musical palette.

In the musical theatre of America, there have been very few composers who have taken advantage of that choice. George Gershwin, Kurt Weill, and Leonard Bernstein come to mind as the exceptions who have dared to be inventive in the use of harmony and melody. Most composers have settled into the language of "pop" harmony which is based on the major-minor scale system peppered with certain predictable chromatic dissonances. That is truly a shame for it has limited the potential of the musical.

One finds this kind of self-imposed stagnation in much of the "pop" musical world. Take a look, for example, at the lyrics of the overwhelming majority of pop tunes. They deal with one subject, romance. Sexual romance, romantic love, conflicts about romance, happy ending romance—it is like going to a supermarket and finding every aisle stocked with chicken. You are reduced to a diet of stewed chicken, fried chicken, chicken soup, chicken gumbo. But, oh, how refreshing if one day there might be vegetables or beef or dairy products to make a balanced diet.

Why we have settled for this state of affairs is a complex question involving economics, politics, and the education of those who both produce and consume popular music. For our purposes here, it is important to note the limitations of music in most musical theatre, and to be aware—as the successes of Gershwin, Weill, and Bernstein have demonstrated—that those limitations are needless.

4. *Inventive use of rhythm.* It is not a sign of good compositional craftsmanship to be limited in the writing of rhythm. Fluctuations of meter, tempo, and individual rhythmic patterns provide the variety which is needed to give composition a satisfying architectural shape. Similarly, the use of syncopation and variations in the frequency with which harmonies change (so-called "harmonic rhythm") can help keep the music from becoming boring. To the extent a composer utilizes all the tools of his rhythmic trade to advantage, his music will be better crafted.

5. *Inventive use of form.* The traditional Tin Pan Alley song is 32 measures in length and is divided into four groups of 8 measures each. An opening melody (the "A section") is played, then repeated with a change of lyric (A¹). A contrasting 8-measure section is then played (the so-called "B section" or "bridge") after which the A section returns with yet another lyric. The AA¹ BA² design is used over and over again in one musical after another. One sees it in "Till There Was You" from *'The Music Man,'* "I Could Have Danced All Night" from *'My Fair Lady,'* "The Heather on the Hill" from *'Brigadoon,'* and dozens more with perhaps a slight variation here or there.

In and of itself, the 32-bar song form is not offensive. What is offensive to the craft-conscious composer is the repetition of the form to the exclusion of other designs which could provide variety in the musical score. To the extent a composer becomes a slave to these overworked formal designs, the music becomes trite. Inventive formal design helps lift a prosaic work to levels of greater craftsmanship.

6. *Use of counterpoint and linear manipulation.* An enormous amount of composition for the musical theatre falls into the category of homophony, that is, a melody supported by underlying chords. Every composer of even casual training knows that there are much more sophisticated techniques for treating a musical line. Lines can be pitted against one another and manipulated in highly imaginative ways. They can be played backward (retrograde), in longer rhythms (augmentation), in shorter rhythms (diminution), and in a kind of intervallic mirror image of their original form (inversion). Each transmutation of the original line can be pitted against the original to form a weave of counterpoint (as the technique is called) which binds a composition into a tremendously unified work of art.

Just as pop music seems to shy away from inventive harmonic systems, it seems to deliberately avoid the sophistications of counterpoint. The use of imitation, augmentation, retrograde, inversion, and all the other techniques one finds in great composers like Bach or Beethoven, Debussy or Stravinsky seems almost deliberately avoided by the likes of Richard Rodgers or Cole Porter, and it is hard to say why. Perhaps the pop composer just doesn't have the ability. Perhaps he doesn't have the desire to become a complete writer. Perhaps he thinks too little of his audience, preferring to believe that compositional sophistication can't be appreciated by the inhabitants of Broadway. Perhaps he is a slave to the publishers and producers who are afraid that only simplistic mediocrity can guarantee a financial return. Perhaps it is a little of each.

In judging the craftsmanship of a musical, however, the presence of contrapuntal technique is certainly a plus, no matter what the financial or aesthetic prejudices of producer, audience, or composer.

7. *Thematic integration.* When one analyzes the writing of great composers, one finds that the melodies which occur over the course of long works are bound together by common elements. A rhythmic motif, an intervallic twist used in one place surfaces again in another. The textbook example of this integration of themes is Beethoven's Symphony #5 in C minor where the opening rhythmic motif of the first movement (the celebrated three short notes followed by a long note) returns again and again in the themes of the remaining movements. To the extent themes grow out of one another, the composition bears a greater organic unity and shows a higher level of craft. Parts fit more gracefully together as if they were each designed not just for themselves but for the welfare of the whole. The compositional tree seems to make sense in total as well as in part. It is not a freak with the trunk of an oak, the branch of a willow, and the leaf of an evergreen.

8. *The integration of musical style with dramatic ambiance.* One does not play baseball in a tuxedo. The tuxedo will not function well to meet the physical demands of the game. The outfit must match the environment. So, too, with the music of the theatre. The character of the music must fit the character of the drama. It would be difficult for *'Gypsy'* to project the image of a burlesque strip joint with music befitting a Tschaikowsky ballet. Elementary as it seems compositional excellence requires a melding of musical and theatrical moods.

9. *Orchestrational quality.* Sid Ramin, Robert Russell Bennett, Phil Lang— who really knows their names? Yet they are the geniuses behind all those great Broadway scores. Richard Rodgers was absolutely dependent upon Robert Russell Bennett to give full effect to his melodies. The great crescendos of *'South Pacific'* and *'My Fair Lady'* are as much Bennett's as Rodgers's or Fritz Loewe's. It is to the eternal shame of many Broadway composers that they are not only incapable of orchestrating their own works but also reluctant to publicly acknowledge those who do.

The quality of orchestration is to be judged not just by how beautifully the instruments are used to paint musical color and mood, but also by how skillfully they allow both spoken and sung voices to project to the listener. Orchestrational craftsmanship is a key element in evaluating the music of the theatre.

10. *The effective use of music not intended for singing.* Melodies which underscore dialogue, overtures which set the mood of a musical and allow latecomers the grace of a few minutes to take their seats, dances which augment the spirit and scope of a production are all important in the non-singing use of music. If handled so that they highlight rather than intrude upon the moment, they can help lift the musical craft to ever higher levels. The evaluation of the composition of a production must

inevitably deal with them as necessary adjuncts to that part of the score which is sung.

Suggested activities

1. Using the information in this section, do a comparative analysis of *'West Side Story'* and *'Grease.'* Why is it that the former is regarded as so much better than the latter in terms of musical craftsmanship?

2. Why do you think the craftsmanship of the "serious" composer has been so lacking in the American musical? What might the consequences be if that craft were more consistently applied?

3. Pick a musical of your own choice and discuss what about its music is well-done and what is poorly done. Be prepared to defend your position on analytical rather than personal grounds. Remember, you are not discussing what you like or don't like but what you think is well-written or poorly written.

Four signs of a well-crafted lyric. The last area we shall investigate in evaluating the quality of writing in a musical is the crafting of the lyric. Here there are four major areas which will concern us, and we will consider each in turn.

1. *Effective transitions from speech to song.* The musical theatre carries with it a literary burden which the normal dramatic work by definition avoids. In a straight drama, the depiction of representational events and characters always occurs in the same way that it does in real life—through speech and action. People talk and interact in the real world; they talk and interact in the dramatic world. The audience easily accepts the latter because it is a mirroring of the former.

Not so in a musical. Speech and action on the musical stage are joined by song, and while song can intensify expression on the one hand, it by definition destroys the illusion of reality on the other. In the real world, no one but the insane sings to communicate—with the possible exception of certain events like a mother humming a lullaby to her baby or someone providing music at a special ceremony like a wedding or coronation or funeral. In the normal course of communication, speech, not song, is the medium of expression.

This state of affairs presents a very delicate paradox for the writers of musical theatre. On the one hand, they need to provide a depiction of real people in believable situations. On the other, they must do so through a medium which clearly contradicts reality. The paradox is solved when the writer learns to effect a smooth transition from the reality of speech to the fantasy of song. In effect, he guides the viewer so gently into another dimension of communication that the new manner of expression is accepted as valid. To understand how this is done, we must first understand something of rhythm and the kinds of verbal communication which rhythm allows.

Some definitions, if you will. Pulse is the uniform division of time, a regular ongoing beat which underlies the music, and against which the surface flow of rhythms is played out. Tempo is the speed at which the pulse travels. Meter is the grouping of pulses by the placement of accents at regular intervals (or sometimes irregular intervals) along the pulse stream. In a waltz, for example, one of every three pulses is accented. In a march, accents are placed on every two or every four pulses. Rhythm is the specific pattern made by the flow of each sound as it occurs. Rhythms in music generally occur against an underlying pulse and meter, although neither pulse nor meter is necessary for the existence of rhythm. Every sound produces a rhythm whether or not a uniform beat is present.

Let's illustrate the concepts above briefly with the use of a familiar nursery rhyme, "Mary had a little lamb." When we say the rhyme, we place regular accents along the way. "*Mary* had a *little* lamb, *little* lamb, *little* lamb. *Mary* had a *little* lamb; its *fleece* was white as *snow*." These accents correspond to the background pulse. There are two subordinate beats between each pulse, and because that number (two) never changes, the pattern produces what is called a duple meter. The rhythm of the words is the actual flow of each syllable as it occurs. "Ma-ry had a lit-tle lamb," etc.

With this understanding of basic rhythmic concepts, it is now possible to define different modes which help make the transition from speech to song.

Everyday speech.   Normal speech is an unmetered, unpulsed flow of words which, though it possesses a surface rhythm, has no regular, recurrent underlying accents to order that rhythm.

Metered speech.   This is a flow of words which contains recurrent accents and pulse groupings. Adding meter to speech is the principle element in distinguishing prose from poetry. Poetry may or may not contain recurrent rhymes, but in order to differentiate itself from prose, it must contain some recurrent pulse or meter.

Recitative.   Recitative is speech which is intoned on only one or two pitches. It may or may not contain an underlying pulse or meter.

Arioso.   Arioso is metered speech with melodic lines which are not extended in time. It is a kind of hybrid between recitative and full-blown melody.

Aria.   An aria is an extended melody in which pulse and meter, rhyme scheme, and instrumental accompaniment are almost always present, and present to a great degree.

As one progresses amid these modes of verbal communication, along the continuum from everyday speech to full-blown aria, one moves ever increasingly from reality of expression to fantasy. The best writers of lyrics understand this and try to move their audiences gracefully from the one to the other. The classic example of how this can be done is the "Seventy-Six Trombones" number from Meredith Willson's '*The Music Man.*'

The number begins with con artist Harold Hill addressing Mr. Dunlop, one of the prominent citizens of River City, Iowa. "Either you are closing your eyes to a situation you do not wish to acknowledge," Hill says, "or you are not aware of the calibre of disaster indicated by the presence of a pool table in your community." His speech is unmetered, everyday prose—but not for long.

"Well, ya got trouble, my friend," Hill continues, and on the word "trouble," an E-flat major scale begins its descent in the orchestra and a duple meter and sharply accented pulse appear. "I say, trouble right here in River City. Why, sure, I'm a billiard player. Mighty proud to say—I'm always mighty proud to say it," Hill goes on, but now his speech is shaped to the pulse and meter of the orchestra. He talks in note values which are written in the musical score to indicate precise rhythms but no pitches.

After awhile, on the words "And the next thing ya know, your son is playing for money in a pinch-back suit," Hill begins to sing his lines on one note. We have now been eased into a recitative. Further along in the number, the recitative grows into arioso when the chorus (the townspeople of River City) sing a response to Hill's exhortation. "Oh, we got trouble!," they sing. "Right here in River City."

The song continues with Hill drifting between metered speech, recitative, and arioso, until, finally, he explodes in a crescendo of flimflam with a full-blown, extended melody. "Seventy-six trombones led the big parade," he sings, "with a hundred-and-ten cornets close behind." Eventually, the chorus joins him in song, and by this time the audience has been so swept up in the architecture and craft of the music and lyrics that it seems as common to sing about the youth of River City as to breathe.

Not every musical number effects a transition from speech to song by going through each mode of verbal expression. What happens in *'The Music Man'* is, after all, an elaborate and lengthy procedure which is not applicable to many dramatic situations. There is, therefore, a shorter mechanism available to the writer which helps accomplish the same goal. That mechanism is the interspersion of dialogue and song. Act I, Scene 1 of *'Oklahoma!'* is a classic example and was one of the musicals which pioneered in the technique.

The scene starts with Aunt Eller churning butter on stage and Curley singing the opening lines of "Oh, What a Beautiful Mornin' " off stage. Presently, Curley appears and there is dialogue which begins to establish characters, relationship, and conflicts. In short order, Laurie enters. Her dialogue with Curley settles into the subject of their upcoming date, the fantasizing of which leads both of them into the song "Surrey with the Fringe on Top." Now the scene continues with the arrival of more characters and the interspersion of yet more dialogue and yet more song.

The net result of all this is to render singing as acceptable a way of communicating as speaking. The trick to using the technique (and Hammerstein was a master of it) is not to alternate song and speech to such an extent that each becomes fragmentary and loses its effect.

2. *Integrating character and lyric.*   Earlier, in our discussion of characterization, we saw the importance of maintaining one's identity in song as well as speech. It is the writer who makes that possible by using lyrics which are tailored to the idiosyncracies of the individual uttering them. The vocabulary and imagery placed in the mouth of a character should fit the nature of that character, and in the best lyrics of the musical stage, they do. The classic example of the technique, as we have mentioned before, is the lyrics of Eliza Doolittle in *'My Fair Lady.'* The cockney regionalisms and images she uses early in the production in songs like "Just You Wait" and "Wouldn't It Be Loverly" help to establish her as a lower class urchin with little education. In "The Rain in Spain" we see a transition not only of pronunciation but of phraseology which indicates that Eliza is gaining in educational stature.

By the time she sings "Without You," she is not only pronouncing words flawlessly but making reference to things as esoteric as the poetry of Keats.

3. *Integrating song and action.* In order to keep the dramatic pace of a musical going and to aid the audience in accepting song as a dramatically valid form of communication, it behooves the writer to allow his lyric to advance the action rather than merely comment upon it. If Mr. Hero turns to Miss Heroine and says in five minutes of flowery dialogue "I am falling in love with you," it becomes dramatically stagnant for him to then sing "I love you" for another five minutes. Better to eliminate the dialogue and let the song deliver the message. In this way, the music and lyrics avoid redundancy and carry the action forward on their own.

The exposition of new material is not the only way that lyrics can integrate with action. Sometimes a bit of "stage business" can spell the difference between a dull musical number and one which is alive. Consider the following example.

The "Matchmaker" song from *'Fiddler'* takes place in Tevye's house and is a kind of romantic fantasizing about marriage carried on by Tevye's five daughters. Even though the music and lyrics themselves are well-crafted, the length of the number requires something more than just singing it. An intelligent staging of it might integrate it with the chores the girls do as they fantasize. A sweep of a broom, a peeling of a potato, etc. can help animate the number and bring it into the fold of the drama, so to speak.

Such integration, of course, can be effected by the director or even the actor himself. To the extent that the writer is aware of the technique, however, he can actually include it in his work so that it is not an element left to chance.

4. *Inventive imagery and poetry.* Finally, good lyrics are those which, on the one hand, use inventive (as opposed to trite) imagery and rhyme when they are called for, and which, on the other, know when to avoid the stuff. There are few lyricists in the history of the musical theatre more adroit than Stephen Sondheim in this regard, and it might serve well to look at two examples of his work which illustrate the principles of originality and simplicity.

At one point in *'Gypsy,'* sisters June and Louise are mercifully left alone by their neurotic mother. They take the opportunity to wish in song that Momma substitute a normal marriage for their chaotic life in the theatre. "If Momma was married, we'd live in a house as private as private can be," they sing. "Just Momma, three ducks, five canaries, a mouse, two monkeys, one father, six turtles, and me. If Momma was married." Sondheim masterfully captures the flavor of children and poignantly juxtaposes their animal references with the longing for a father and stability. That he does this all in an essentially humorous song is a wonderful example of the use of comedy to effect the revelation of a family tragedy.

But his cleverness is hardly exhausted. Consider the following sequence of imaginative references and rhyme schemes which occur later in the number. "Momma, please take our advice. We aren't the Lunts. I'm (June singing) not Fanny Bryce. Momma, we'll buy you the rice, if only this once you wouldn't think twice. It could be so nice, if Momma got married to stay," etc.

Sondheim can obviously turn it on with the best of them, but even more to his credit, he knows when to turn it off, when to cease the cute literary phrase and make his effect with simplicity. Consider his impeccable lyrical judgment in "Somewhere" from *'West Side Story.'* Tony and Maria are in love. They long for an environment in which racial harmony might allow that love to live, and in their song, they express that longing, not in flowery poetry or fancy rhyme schemes, but in a simple, unaffected statement which gives majesty to their plea. "There's a place for us," they sing, "somewhere a place for us. Hold my hand and we're halfway there. Hold my hand and I'll take you there. Somehow. Someday. Somewhere."

Judgments like Sondheim's are rarely taught. They are more often an innate spark of insight cultivated internally by the craftsman. The evaluator must know how to assess them, the aspiring artist how to appreciate and emulate them.

Suggested activities

1.   The lyrics of *'Gypsy'* and *'West Side Story'* are monuments of the musical theatre. So are those of *'My Fair Lady.'* Read them, study them, and discuss how they reveal the four signs of excellence above.

2.   The lyrics of *'The Fantasticks'* are unusual because of the allegorical nature of the drama. Compare them to the lyrics of the musicals above. Do they successfully meet the four criteria of good lyric writing? If so, why? If not, why not?

3.   Choose a musical whose lyrics you think are less than successful and discuss why you hold that opinion. Select a song from that musical and suggest how the lyrics might be improved upon.

PART IV

Trying Your Hand

INTRODUCTORY REMARKS

Now that you have absorbed something of the history and repertoire of your art form, now that you have familiarized yourself with the elements of production and critical evaluation, it is time to try your own hand at creating and staging a piece of musical theatre. In taking on this project, let us agree to some ground rules and a course of action before we proceed. Since the writing of most musicals has involved converting a novel or preexisting play, let us agree to base our work on material already available rather than an original story. For our purposes here, that will be a far easier and more pedagogically prudent course. In choosing this course, let us further agree to review some of the elements used in converting one literary medium to another so that we prepare the way for our creative effort. With this approach in mind, our work will proceed in five stages:

A.   A brief discussion of the differences between certain literary media.

B.   A brief discussion of the specific elements involved in converting existing material to the musical stage.

C.   A look at an example of media conversion.

D.   Suggested assignments for your own work.

A. THE DIFFERENCES BETWEEN MEDIA

If eventually we are going to take an existing film or novel and turn it into a musical play, we need to be aware of the technical differences between one literary medium and another which will affect both our writing and the demands made upon our performers. The most crucial of these differences as far as the writing is concerned is the presentation of time, the choice of location, and the utilization of space.

Whereas a novel can be played out in the mind of the reader, whereas a film can project the panorama of a camera, the stage is limited by its own physical dimensions and the technical resources of its sets and props. For this reason, the number of locations, amount of space required for realizing action, number of separate scenes, and portrayal of the passage of time are a good deal more limited for the stage than for either the novel or film. Let us consider some examples of this precept.

The opening of the film version of *'The Sound of Music'* shows Julie Andrews standing amid the meadowed ridges of the Austrian Alps. The grandeur and space of the location of the drama are presented instantly and to a degree that no stage set could possibly match. Later in Act I of the stage version, Max looks out over the audience to an imagined landscape and asks who lives in this castle and that. The audience must accept the fact that they cannot see the landscape. For the moment, they view it only through Max's description and their own imagination. Not so in the film, for there the camera can instantly assume the function of Max's eye and, indeed, the eye of every member of the audience. Max points to a town, a valley, a mountain peak, and presto—the film is edited to show us what he sees.

In the same way the stage is limited in presenting the panorama of a location, it is limited by both the speed with which one location becomes another and the number of locations which can be depicted. Read Michener's *Tales of the South Pacific* or view the movie version of *'South Pacific,'* and with the speed of the imagination or flick of a camera lens, one can be at Emile's plantation, the island of Bali Ha'i, the American military compound, or an embattled South Sea war zone. On the stage, such changes must occur more slowly, and by force of the physical limitations of set design, there must be fewer of them.

Then, too, the passage of time cannot be as easily depicted on stage as in a film or novel. It is true that lighting can dissolve an evening into a morning in the theatre nearly as fast as on the screen, but what of dissolving a winter into a spring? In the movie version of Robert Bolt's *A Man for All Seasons,* for example, one sees the length of Thomas Moore's imprisonment by following the leaves of the tree outside Moore's cell as they bloom, wither, decay, and re-blossom again. In the original play, Bolt has to communicate this passage of time with dialogue which is more lengthy and less visual. In *'My Fair Lady,'* Lerner and Loewe require an entire time-passage scene (Act I, Scene 6) to show Eliza's progress in learning to speak. A novelist could accomplish the same thing (though with different impact) in a sentence or two.

The effect of differences like these upon both actor and writer is considerable. The camera, for example, can zoom in to pick up a gesture as small as the curl of a lip or twitch of an eye brow. It can pull back to render a character inconspicuous against an enormous panorama. The celluloid actor, then, has a variety of techniques for building characterization, ranging from exquisitely subtle to incredibly broad. He can whisper or shout, work his physical being in minute or exaggerated proportions—all depending upon the angle of the camera. The stage actor must constantly tailor himself to the unchanging dimensions of the theatre itself. Whispers can never be so soft as to be inaudible in the back of the hall. Gestures can neither be so small that they go unseen by a viewer in the balcony nor so large that they become a burlesque. The writer must know all these things and adjust his stage directions and lines accordingly.

There are other significant effects which media differences have upon both actors and writers. In the celluloid world of motion pictures and television, for example, finances dictate that scenes be shot out of order. If a movie script calls for, say, desert locations and mountain locations, all the desert scenes will be shot before cast and crew travel to the mountains. The interspersion of desert and mountain scenes is done in the editing room, not by the actor in actual playing sequence. On the stage, even though a given rehearsal may center upon only one scene or hop from scene to scene, in performance the scenes follow in actual sequence and the actor gets a sense of the continuity of the script. He can build his mood and character in an order approximating reality. The celluloid actor has to be able to recall various emotions, lines, and gestures out of sequence according to the vagaries of a shooting schedule.

Then there is the matter of the final product. The film, once made, is made—irrevocable, unchangeable. Stage works, hopefully, run through many performances, and, over the course of a run, the actor can continue to expand and develop his character. He must also keep from being bored by the repetition of the same performance night after night, and that almost necessitates little changes or tricks which help keep a character fresh and a mind concentrated on business.

All this and more must be accounted for by the writer who seeks to convert existing material from another medium to the musical stage—and that is even before the obvious considerations of replacing dialogue and action with song and dance.

B. ELEMENTS OF MEDIA CONVERSION

Bearing in mind the differences between media, there are four very specific things the writer can do in adapting existing material to the musical stage. They are: capsuling time and events; limiting characters to a dramatically reasonable number; using dialogue and action to replace descriptive narration; and using song and dance to expand reality. Let us consider each in turn.

Capsuling time and events. The writer of musical theatre must be able to tell his story with an economy of scenes. Consider Lionel Bart's problems in converting *Oliver Twist* by Charles Dickens into the musical *'Oliver.'* The novel begins with Oliver's birth and spans a period of ten or eleven years, the early years of Oliver's boyhood. There are dozens upon dozens of separate locations and events in Dickens's unfolding of the story. Bart's task (and he did it well) was to pick only those events and that time frame essential to the plot so that he could tell it within the structural confines of a two-act musical which could play in two or two-and-a-half hours.

Limiting the number of characters. A film can use a limitless stream of actors to tell its story. A town, for example, can be a whole town—a real town—of hundreds or even thousands of people. The stage is a good deal more limited in space and in the financial resources of the producer. There is no such thing as a musical with the proverbial "cast of thousands." Characters, then, must be chosen for their centrality to a story, and often several characters of a film or novel have to be capsulized into one stage character.

Using dialogue and action to replace written narrative. When converting a novel or short story to a musical, the development of character and unfolding of plot, which often take place as a descriptive narration in the former, must be shown as a visual event in the latter. The classic examples of this principle are, of course, the conversions of Cervantes's *Don Quixote* to *'Man of La Mancha'* and Dickens's *Oliver Twist* to *'Oliver.'* When Cervantes describes the appearance of Don Quixote, or Dickens sets the mood of Fagin's den of thieves, with a paragraph or page of great prose, they by definition draw upon a literary technique which is designed to stimulate the imagination of the reader. The reader is called upon to complete the process of communication between himself and the author by supplying his own mental picture of the words he reads. In the theatre, the dramatist must supply the picture itself. What a character *does,* the words he says, the acts he commits, his walk, his dress—all this must substitute for the prose of the novelist. The set and lighting must convey the dramatic ambiance in a glance where once the novelist could do it with description. We *see* the squalor of Fagin's lair because it is dimly lit, painted in dark hues, and made to look decrepid.

The use of song and dance to expand reality. Finally, the writers of musical theatre must know how and when to replace the speech and action of novel, film, or play with music, lyric, and choreography. We have already discussed the delicate paradox of this undertaking: the expansion of reality by things not part of reality. What we consider now is not so much the "how" of the problem but the "when" of it.

"When" during the story is it appropriate to break the parameters of conventional communication and insert underdialogue music or song or dance? There are no pat answers to this question, but there is a guiding principle. Whenever the level of emotion needs intensification, the fantasy of musical communication (if correctly handled) can provide it. There are few examples clearer than the opening of *'South Pacific'* when Emile and Nellie wonder what it would be like to fall in love.

We have all been there, yes? We can all recall that moment when we looked into the eyes of a stranger to whom we were attracted and asked ourselves, "what would it be like to fall in love with that person over there?" What occurs to us as a fleeting thought in reality is expanded by Rodgers and Hammerstein into an unforgettable scene. The lights dim on Emile. He freezes. Nellie is hit with a spot, and we realize that we are not in representational time, but in the fantasy of Nellie's thoughts. "Wonder how I'd feel," she sings, "living on a hillside, looking on an ocean, beautiful and still." She freezes. The light on her dims. A second spot comes up full on Emile. We are now visualizing his thoughts. "This is what I've longed for. Someone young and smiling, climbing up my hill." Back and forth we go between the two as each probes the possibilities of establishing a romantic relationship. Finally, the spots join, both characters resume the action of real time, and the dialogue of representational drama continues.

It is not only the way in which the authors treat the music and lyrics which makes this one of the great moments in all musical theatre. It is the astuteness of their judgment in selecting this moment above others. Again, the guide is a desire for intensification. What might have happened in a novel in a sentence or two, what might have been expressed in a film or a play as a glance or passing word between characters, is now unfolded in much more time and with the impact of music. The event is expanded in its proportions and its meaning. The emotions of the characters are revealed with much greater intensity, and that cannot fail to transfer to the audience.

Suggested activities

1. At this point it might be profitable to analyze in depth the examples discussed above. Choose *Don Quixote, Oliver Twist, Tales of the South Pacific,* or *Romeo and Juliet* and discuss how each was transformed into its musical (*'Man of La Mancha,' 'Oliver,' 'South Pacific,' 'West Side Story,'* respectively). How did the authors of the musicals account for the differences in media? How did they handle the elements of media conversion discussed above?

2. Pick a scene from a film, play, story, or novel of your own choice. Discuss how you might transform it into a musical. What would you have to do in capsuling characters, capsuling time, or replacing narrative with visual theatre? Where would you insert music, song, or dance? Be prepared to defend your choices with good theatrical logic.

C. AN EXAMPLE OF MEDIA CONVERSION

On one or two occasions in the pages above, we have mentioned *A Tale of Two Cities,* the great romantic epic by Charles Dickens set against the panoply of the French Revolution. The story meets every criteria for a profound theatrical libretto and offers an excellent opportunity to study the adaptation of a novel to the stage. Let us see how the technique works by taking one scene from the novel and transforming it to the medium of musical theatre.

The scene we shall study comes from the sixth chapter of Dickens's book, a chapter he entitles "The Shoemaker." We can set the stage for the scene by describing the characters who will appear in our musical adaptation. In order of appearance, they are:

1. *Dr. Alexander Manette.* Once a physician in the service of the French nobility, Dr. Manette has been imprisoned by the nobility for nearly twenty years for crimes he has never committed. During this time, his wife has died, and his young daughter, Lucy, whom he barely remembers, has grown to womanhood. He himself has become deranged by the hardship of his confinement. Now, on the eve of the French Revolution, his daughter has returned to France from her home in England to rescue her father with the help of British friends and the French revolutionary underground.

2. *John Barsad.* Barsad is the jailor of Dr. Manette's section of the prison. He is a mercenary ne'er-do-well always ready to sell his services as a spy to the highest bidder. On this occasion, he has been bribed to leave the door to Manette's cell ajar.

3. *Ernst DeFarge.* DeFarge is one of the leaders of the French revolutionary underground. He is a wine merchant who, along with his wife, Theresa, plots the overthrow of the French aristocracy.

4. *Lucy Manette.* The doctor's daughter, now grown, is determined not only to rescue her father but to restore him to mental and physical health.

5. *C.J. Stryver.* Stryver is a British lawyer with political ties and friends in the French underground. It is through his contacts that the doctor's rescue is being effected.

6. *Charles Darnay.* Darney is a French aristocrat who hates the aristocracy and has renounced his own legal and financial claims to it. He now resides in London where, besides teaching French, he helps Stryver's law firm in the rescue of innocent people like Manette. Eventually, he and Lucy will fall in love and marry.

7. *Sidney Carton.* Carton is the hero of the story. He is Stryver's law partner, brilliant and witty. He is also an alcoholic who has never been able to realize his potential. In this scene, he is drunk. Eventually, he, too, falls in love with Lucy,

and when he realizes that he will never have her, he gives up his life to save her husband, Darnay.

In the novel, Dickens begins the scene with a description of Dr. Manette. During his years of confinement, Manette has taken up shoemaking to pass the time. DeFarge comes to the cell door and asks the doctor if he is working. "Yes—I am working," Manette replies, and Dickens writes the following:

> "The faintness of the voice was pitiable and dreadful. It was not the faintness of physical weakness, though confinement and hard fare no doubt had their part in it. Its deplorable peculiarity was that it was the faintness of solitude and disuse. It was like the last feeble echo of a sound made long ago. So entirely had it lost the life and resonance of the human voice, that it affected the senses like a once beautiful color faded away into a poor, weak stain. So sunken and suppressed it was, that it was like a voice underground. So expressive it was of a hopeless and lost creature, that a famished traveler, wearied out by lonely wandering in a wilderness, would have remembered home and friends in such a tone before lying down to die."

After the description, one by one the rescue party unsuccessfully tries to draw the old doctor into conversation. His mind is nearly gone, however, and he is capable of only brief responses before returning to work feebly at his shoes. Then Dickens has Lucy step forward, and through the bonds of blood and love which span their twenty years of separation, she begins to stir her father. Again, Dickens writes:

> "Not yet trusting the tones of her voice, she sat down on the bench beside him. He recoiled, but she lay her hand upon his arm. A strange thrill struck him when she did so and visibly passed over his frame. He laid the knife down softly as he sat staring at her...She held him close round the neck and rocked him on her breast like a child...a sight so touching, yet so terrible in the tremendous wrong and suffering which had gone before it...Then, in the submissive way of one long accustomed to obey under coercion...he put on the cloak and wrappings that they gave him to wear. He readily responded to his daughter's drawing her arm through his, and took—and kept—her hand in both his own. They began to descend..."

If ever a scene were suited to musical adaptation it is this scene. The emotional level of it is deep, and even Dickens's own narration focuses in on the aural as well as the visual. The forlornness of Manette's voice, the contrasting strength of Lucy's are just made for musical expression. Consider, now, the musical adaptation of this scene below.*

(A single ray of light coming from above rises slowly on cell #105, North Tower, Bastille. Outside the cell door stands JOHN BARSAD, turnkey. Inside, sitting at a makeshift cobbler's bench, is DR. ALEXANDER MANETTE. He has an unfinished shoe before him along with miscellaneous tools and scraps of material. He is a man of sixty who bears the physical and emotional scars of twenty years of solitary confinement. There is music under.)

MANETTE

(To BARSAD)   Have you seen my leather?...

(BARSAD ignores him, glances at his watch and exits. MANETTE searches among his scraps and finds a piece of leather.)

Ah...now...the needle...

(He takes up his sewing and begins to work. The music becomes more rhythmic. Mechanically and with a forlorn voice, he sings.)

I TAKE MY THREAD AND DRAW IT SO...
I TIE IT FAST AS I HAVE DONE BEFORE...
IT IS THE ONLY WORK I KNOW...
AND IT SHALL LAST...
UNTIL I SEE MY HOME ONCE MORE.

(The orchestra picks up his strain and continues it while he hums intermittently, buried in his work. BARSAD returns accompanied by STRYVER, DARNAY, LUCY, CARTON, and DEFARGE. DARNAY takes out a wallet and hands BARSAD a clip of money. BARSAD gives DARNAY his keys, shakes his hand, and exits. DARNAY unlocks the door. MANETTE is now aware of their presence but continues to look only at his work. The music fades into the dialogue.)

DEFARGE

(From the doorway)   Good day.

MANETTE

(Still looking down at his work)   Good day...

DEFARGE

You are hard at work, I see.

MANETTE

Yes... I am working...

---

*The adaptation is excerpted from *THE BEST OF TIMES*, book by Corey Pepper and Steven Porter, music and lyrics by Steven Porter. It is reprinted here by permission of the authors.

DEFARGE

I want to let in more light. Can you bear a little more?

MANETTE

(Looking up)   What did you say?...

CARTON

(Impulsively, from the doorway)   He wants to let in more light.

STRYVER

(Whispering)   Sh!   Sidney!

DEFARGE

I say, can you bear more light?

MANETTE

I must bear it, if you let it in...

     (DEFARGE crosses to the window, then to MANETTE who has resumed his work.)

DEFARGE

Are you going to finish that pair of shoes today?

MANETTE

What did you say?

DEFARGE

Do you mean to finish that pair of shoes today?

MANETTE

I can't say that I mean to...I suppose so...I don't know...

DEFARGE

You have visitors. You see?   (He motions to STRYVER and DARNAY.)   Come.

    (They step forward.)

STRYVER

Good day, Monsieur. (Pause. No reaction.)   It is a lovely shoe you have there.   Who made it?

MANETTE

(Looking up again)   Did you ask my name?...

STRYVER

Assuredly, sir. I did.

MANETTE

One hundred five...North Tower...

DEFARGE

Is that all?

MANETTE

One hundred five...North Tower...

(He resumes his work. DARNAY steps to him.)

DARNAY

You are not a shoemaker by trade?

MANETTE

(Turning to the new voice) I am not a shoemaker by trade?...No...I am not a shoemaker by trade. I...I learned it here. I taught myself. I asked leave to...(His thoughts trail away, and he goes back to his sewing.) I asked leave to teach myself, and I got it with much difficulty after a very long time...And I have made shoes ever since.

CARTON

(Impatiently) Dr. Manette, do you remember nothing of Monsieur Stryver?

STRYVER

(Annoyed) Sidney, please!

LUCY

(Crossing to her father) Wherever you learned, Monsieur, it is a beautiful shoe.

(The others are startled by her manner. They retreat, leaving her alone with MANETTE.)

MANETTE

What did you say?...

LUCY

It is a beautiful shoe. Will you show me how you did it?

(Music under)

MANETTE

(Singing) I TAKE MY THREAD...

LUCY

(Singing) YOU TAKE YOUR THREAD...

MANETTE

AND DRAW IT SO...

LUCY

AND DRAW IT SO...

BOTH

AND TIE IT FAST
AS YOU (I) HAVE DONE BEFORE...

(LUCY takes the work from his hands as if from a child's and begins to pack his things as she continues the song. Fascinated by her gentleness and the strength of her aria, MANETTE watches her in silence.)

LUCY

I KNOW THAT IT IS ALL YOU KNOW
BUT THAT IS PAST NOW,
THAT IS PAST NOW.
AND I CAN SEE A BETTER PLACE
BEYOND THESE WALLS, BEYOND THIS DOOR,
WHERE YOU WILL WALK AMONG YOUR FELLOW MAN
AS YOU HAVE DONE.
AND YOU WILL KNOW
THE THINGS THAT YOU HAVE ALWAYS KNOWN BEFORE.

(The music continues under as LUCY SPEAKS.) I know a place where you can make shoes even more beautiful than these.   Would you like that?

MANETTE

I suppose so...

STRYVER

Pardon me, but is he fit for the journey?

DEFARGE

More fit for that, I think, than to remain here.

STRYVER

In that case, it is business, Monsieur, and we had better arrange for a coach.

(He exists, taking CARTON and the others with him. LUCY and MAN-NETTE are now alone. LUCY picks up her father's tools and places her shawl on his shoulders. MANETTE is somewhat frightened. He turns to her.)

MANETTE

May I hold my work, please?

(LUCY gives him his unfinished shoe and takes his hand as she guides him towards the cell door.)

LUCY

(Singing)
> COME TAKE MY HAND
> AND HOLD IT SO
> AND LET US WALK BEYOND THIS PRISON DOOR
> IT IS A FAR, FAR BETTER PLACE
> TO WHICH WE GO...

MANETTE

I knew a lawyer once by the name of Stryver...in London...

LUCY

(Speaking) Yes. Yes. In London! (She finishes the song as they exit.)

THAN YOU HAVE EVER KNOWN BEFORE.

(The lights dim on an empty cell.)

Scene 2. The Cobbler's Song. A Better Place

(LUCY: It is a beautiful shoe...)

(Dialogue: LUCY: I know a place...)

Suggested activities

Read the opening of the Dickens novel and compare his Chapter Six to the setting above by answering the following questions:

1. Are there any "capsuled" characters in the musical setting?   If so, who and why?

2. Describe what has been altered in the musical setting from the original text. What action has been eliminated? What dialogue has been changed, etc.?

3. The original scene is not set in a jail cell but rather a garret where DeFarge has hidden Manette. Why has this been changed?

4. Reading to the end of the novel, what similarities in location and dialogue do you find between this scene and Carton's last thoughts of Lucy? Might the song in this scene be reprised later?

5. Analyze and criticize the scene using the knowledge of writing and media conversion you have gained in the pages above.

D. SUGGESTED ASSIGNMENTS

There is so much great literature from which to choose in making adaptations for the musical stage that one hardly knows where to begin. The suggestions below are only that—suggestions. Feel free to substitute any worthy piece of writing for the assignments given here.

A word on literary form before you begin your writing. Note the various conventions used in setting a musical down on the written page. Characters are capitalized, as are lyrics—which are also indented to distinguish them easily from what is spoken. Stage directions are written in parentheses. The character speaking is identified in capitals at the center of the page. His words appear below beginning at the left margin. Be sure to note when any proposed music begins and ends.

Some novels suitable for media conversion:

1.   *To Kill a Mockingbird* by Harper Lee is a tale of the American South, profound and humorous, poignant and loving. It is essentially the story of Jem, a young white girl, who matures as her father defends an innocent black man in a town bent on hanging him. There are many chapters which lend themselves readily to musical adaptation, but you might consider the one in which Jem finally confronts her retarded next-door neighbor, Boo Radley, as a human being worthy of her respect. It might be useful to note that *To Kill a Mockingbird* was adapted into a critically acclaimed motion picture, one of actor Gregory Peck's finest.

2.   *Billy Budd* by Herman Melville. In Melville you will be dealing with one of the greatest novelists in the history of the English language, and in *Billy Budd* you will be dealing with a semi-allegorical tale of good and evil set against the story of nineteenth century men at sea. There is a moment in the novel when Billy, the personification of good, and Claggart, the personification of evil, converse. It would be interesting to set that moment musically. You may wish to know that the novel was made into a rather fine movie and that Benjamin Britten, the great twentieth century composer, set it as an opera.

3.   Pearl S. Buck's *The Good Earth,* also made into a much heralded motion picture, is a tale of social evolution and human values set in China. There are many scenes of humor and tragedy to choose for a musical rendering. Select any you wish, and be aware that you may be more comfortable changing the location of the novel to fit your musical style. When Rodgers and Hammerstein decided to adapt Molnar's *Liliom* to produce *'Carousel,'* they changed locations from Eastern Europe to New England. It was a background more compatible with their own writing style and one which generated speech and song more accessible to an American audience. There is no mandate to change Pearl Buck's location, but the possibility exists. Just remember that in exercising it you must maintain the integrity of her action, characters, and

119.

themes.

4. *The Keys to the Kingdom* by A.J. Cronin si the heartwarming tale of the life of a priest as he grows to maturity first in a Scottish seminary and then as a missionary in China. Again, to help you in your media conversion, you might wish to view the film version of the novel. The farewell scene when Father Francis, now an old man, leaves his Chinese mission to retire in Scotland would make a touching full-cast finale. You might consider it for your work. In the case of this novel, it might be wise to leave the geography where it is, since it is in the juxtaposing of Father Francis, a white European, with the culture of China that Cronin achieves much of his humor and tenderness.

5. George Eliot's *Silas Marner* is one of the classics of the English language. It is the story of an old recluse who is spiritually resurrected by the love of a young girl whom he finds abandoned, takes in, and raises as his own. The scene early in the novel when he first encounters the child and must decide whether or not to love her would make a powerful musical soliloquy.

Some plays which might make good musicals:

1. Jean Anouilh's *Beckett* is the story of the love-hate relationship between Thomas Beckett and King Henry II of England. It offers the musical stage a Medieval period piece of splendor and profundity. It is also one of the most powerful stories of love between two men caught in the destructive paradoxes of politics and religion. You may wish to view the splendid film version of the play, but it would be wiser to work directly from Anouilh's script, since that is already tailored to the demands of the stage. There is scarcely a scene which does not lend itself to musical adaptation.

2. *Death of a Salesman* by Arthur Miller is not conventional theatrical fare, although it has certainly become a classic of modern drama. It is offered here because it will give you a chance to set the fantasies of a character to music, a medium which, because it is ideally suited to expand reality, can conveniently depict fantasy. Any of Willy's mental ramblings would make fine musical scenes, but you might particularly consider those in which he fantasizes that his son, Biff, is a big football hero. The brassy, up-tempo lilt of a football fight song peppered with dissonances which indicate Willy's deteriorated state of mind could produce a chilling effect on the musical stage.

3. Garson Kanin's *Born Yesterday* is a wonderful comedy about the educational and spiritual transformation of a gangster's moll into a thinking, caring citizen. The movie version which starred Paul Douglas as the gangster, Judy Holliday as the moll, and William Holden as the reporter who sets the transformation in motion, will give you a fine visualization of the play. There are many scenes from which to choose, but you might consider setting the famous gin rummy game to music.

4. *Our Town* by Thornton Wilder will give you the opportunity to work with allegorical story theatre. The play deals with human values and emotions portrayed in a small American town. The intertwining of lives and events is revealed both by

action and by the dialogue of a narrator whose literary viewpoint is one of omniscience. A song which emanates from the narrator and is transferred to the characters would make for an effective and challenging assignment.

5. Edmond Rostand's *Cyrano de Bergerac* is one of the classics of the stage. Rostand's writing style, witness *'The Fantasticks,'* is readily suited to music, and because Cyrano is a character given to poetry, it would be dramatically very logical to have him given also to song. There is particular appeal in this play since it is a love story without the usual happy endings so predictable in much musical theatre. Two possibilities for solo singing by Cyrano are his speech on the value of "panache" and, of course, his love poem beneath the balcony.

Some motion pictures suitable for musicals:

1. *Mr. Roberts,* the World War II comedy which starred James Cagney, Henry Fonda, and Jack Lemmon, is a natural for a rousing musical with a bittersweet ending. There are many opportunities for solo as well as full-production numbers, and the latter would be an especially good assignment. Girl-starved sailors and romance-starved nurses might produce a pretty lively musical ensemble.

2. *How Green Was My Valley* is one of the greatest films of all time. Set in a Welsh mining town, the film already utilizes Welsh choral music as an integral part of the drama. This tender story of a boy coming of age at a time of social and industrial change could make as powerful a musical as ever graced the stage. There are romamce, social import, humor, and sadness all portrayed with the unforgettable language, poetry, and music of the Welsh people. Pick a scene—any scene—and good musical writing could make it a lasting part of the repertoire.

3. *Lilies of the Field* is the delightful comedy of a black man coming to the aid of impoverished European nuns in a poor desert town in the American Southwest. Sidney Poitier's performance just bristled with humor and song. The opportunities for musical variety here are enormous. You have the potential for hand-clapping black gospel hymns, Old World German folk songs, and the country and western snap of a hoedown. The scene in which Poitier teaches the rhythmically "square" nuns how to sing a down-home spiritual was a gem on the screen and would make a tremendous impact on the stage.

4. *Anastasia* starred Ingrid Bergman, Yul Brynner, and Helen Hayes and told the story of the search for the Princess Anastasia during the years after the Russian Revolution. It would afford the musical writer an opportunity for a poignant personal tale and a very opulent setting. Particularly suited for music is the scene in which Anastasia must prove who she is to the old Dowager.

5. *The Mudlark* is an old movie which also involved royalty. Irene Dunne played the role of Queen Victoria, Alec Guinness, the role of Prime Minister Disraeli. The story involves a young "mudlark," an orphan called Wheeler who survives by selling items he forages from the mud of the Thames. One day Wheeler finds a brooch with the picture of the Queen. He fancies her his mother and manages to sneak into

Windsor Castle to meet her. His genuine love for her helps her to overcome her loneliness for Prince Albert who has recently died. It also gives Disraeli the political impetus to enact the social legislation needed to protect children like Wheeler. The possibilities for music, solo and ensemble, are limitless. You may wish to try your hand at the scene in which Wheeler meets Queen Victoria.

Further assignments. Adaptations are, of course, not the only thing one can do to learn the art of musical stage. Reading the literature about the musical theatre, studying the libretti and scores which make up the repertoire, and performing selected scenes from that repertoire are all indispensable to the well-trained craftsman. The musicals discussed in Part I above and the suggested references given below will help build a sound foundation.

What scenes you can actually produce and what musicals you can actually mount will depend upon the environment in which you read this text. Whatever that environment, I hope you use it to its fullest and that the information here to some degree enables you to do so.

SUGGESTED REFERENCES

Books

1. *The American Musical Theatre.* Lehman Engel (New York: Macmillan, 1975).

2. *The Best Musicals from SHOW BOAT to A CHORUS LINE.* Arthur Jackson (New York: Crown, 1977).

3. *Blacking Up: the minstrel show in nineteenth century America.* Robert C. Toll (New York: Oxford University Press, 1974).

4. *Broadway Musicals.* Martin Gottfried (The Netherlands: Harry N. Abrams, 1979).

5. *Broadway's Greatest Musicals.* Abe Laufe (New York: Funk and Wagnalls, 1970).

6. *Getting To Know Him: a biography of Oscar Hammerstein II.* Hugh Fordin (New York: Random House, 1977).

7. *Great Musicals of the American Theatre.* Stanley Richards, ed. (Radnor, Pa.: Chilton, 1976). Contains the libretti of *LEAVE IT TO ME, LADY IN THE DARK, LOST IN THE STARS, WONDERFUL TOWN, FIORELLO, CAMELOT, MAN OF LA MANCHA, CABARET, APPLAUSE,* and *A LITTLE NIGHT MUSIC.*

8. *Musicals: a directory of properties available for production.* Richard Chigley Lynch (Chicago: American Library Association, 1984).

9. *The New Complete Book of the American Musical Theatre.* David Ewen (New York: Holt, Rinehart, and Winston, 1970).

10. *On with the Show.* Robert C. Toll (New York: Oxford University Press, 1976).

11. *The Rodgers and Hammerstein Fact Book.* Stanley Green, ed. (New York: The Lynn Farnol Group, 1980).

12. *Simon's Directory of Theatrical Materials, Services, and Information.* Bernard Simon, ed. (New York: Package Publicity Service, annually updated).

13. *Six Plays by Rodgers and Hammerstein.* Richard Rodgers and Oscar Hammerstein II (New York: The Modern Library, n.d.). Contains the libretti of *OKLAHOMA!, CAROUSEL, ALLEGRO, SOUTH PACIFIC, THE KING AND I,* and *ME AND JULIET.*

14. *Stagecraft and Scenic Design.* Herbert Philippi (Boston: Houghton Mifflin, 1953).

15. *Sondheim and Co.* Craig Zadan (New York: MacMillan, 1974).

16. *The Street Where I Live.* Alan Jay Lerner (New York: Norton, 1978).

17. *The Story of America's Musical Theatre.* David Ewen (Philadelphia: Chilton, 1961).

18. *Ten Great Musicals of the American Theatre.* Stanley Richards, ed. (Radnor, Pa.: Chilton, 1973). Contains the libretti of *OF THEE I SING, PORGY AND BESS, ONE TOUCH OF VENUS, BRIGADOON, KISS ME, KATE, WEST SIDE STORY, FIDDLER ON THE ROOF, 1776,* and *COMPANY.*

19. *Their Words Are Music: the great theatre lyricists and their lyrics.* Lehman Engel (New York: Crown, 1975).

20. *To the Actor.* Michael Chekhov (New York: Harper and Row, 1953).

21. *The World of Musical Comedy.* Stanley Green (New York: Grosset and Dunlap, 1962).

Recordings and Films

Almost every major opera and musical record and film available as well as audio/visual anthologies and histories of the musical theatre may be obtained from the two suppliers listed below. In addition, their catalogues contain a treasure house of films and recordings of dramatic works, motion pictures, and many fine educational anthologies on the dramatic arts.

—1—

Educational Record Sales (ERS)
157 Chambers St.
New York, N.Y. 10007
(212) 267-7437

—2—

Educational Audio/Visual Materials (EAV)
Pleasantville, N.Y. 10570
(914) 769-6332

INDEX